I0548113

CONTENTS

DISTURBANCE

A Gathering Storm Novella
By
Marlow Kelly

Disturbance
A Gathering Storm Novella

Edited by Corinne Demaagd
From CMD Writing and Editing
https://cmdediting.com

For news of Marlow's next release sign up for Marlow's Newsletter at: www.marlowkelly.com

CHAPTER ONE

Mr. Squint's hands shook as he slid a check across the desk to defense attorney Sophia Reed. She couldn't tell if he was trembling because his son had escaped a prison sentence or if it was caused by the horror of seeing him on the stand.

She placed the payment in her briefcase for deposit later. The action gave her time to consider her next words. Then she eased back in her chair, studying the young man she had just saved from doing jail time. Jason looked like your average high school nerd. He had short mousy-brown hair and thick round glasses that did nothing to hide the grief and pain that shone in his eyes. He glared at her with open contempt, which was not a surprise.

She suspected on the night he was arrested, he had gotten high and crashed the car in a failed suicide attempt. He seemed to be holding on to his hurt and anguish over his mother's sudden death from a heart attack, which was understandable. Unfortunately, his sorrow had morphed into a drinking and drug habit that would not only destroy him, but had the potential to kill innocent bystanders.

In her experience, young angry men didn't listen to reason so she switched her attention to his father, hoping there was some way to get through to them and help them recover. Harlan wasn't coping well with his wife's death either. He was probably in his forties but looked much older. His clothes, much like his skin, hung off his bones, symptoms of a sudden weight loss. Everything about him seemed wrinkled, his posture, his suit, and even his thinning fair hair looked as though they had been crumpled into a big ball that had yet to unfurl.

She took a deep breath and then said, "Harlan, Jason needs help."

Jason's lips curled into a sneer. "Who are you to tell me what I need?"

"Be quiet," Harlan snapped.

Harlan's reaction caught Sophia by surprise. This was the first time he'd censured his son. One glance at Jason's face told her he was equally astonished.

She seized the moment to say her piece. "Jason, you were too drunk to drive, and you admitted as much to the police. It was only an act of God"—*or incompetence*—"that has given you a second chance."

"What do you mean?" The youngster's voice still held a hint of bravado, but he wasn't as confident or aggressive.

"Detective Needham mixed up his cases when he testified. I was fully expecting to have to argue against your admission and your refusal to agree to alcohol testing. I was also planning to bring up your mother's recent demise and convince the judge to suspend imprisonment, in favor of you completing a court-ordered chemical dependency program."

"They couldn't prove I was drunk. I was just tired from studying, and I fell asleep."

In Sophia's opinion, that wasn't much better, but she wasn't going there. Instead, she opened the police report and pointed to the paragraph that proved his guilt. "Quote, 'I've been drinking. Thank God, I didn't kill anyone.' End quote. Jason, try and see this for what it is...a second chance."

"She's right." Harlan seemed to be struggling with his son. She had seen it before. It wasn't that he didn't care, but he was dealing with his own torment and had no idea how to help Jason.

Sophia couldn't say she had an answer on how to cope with such a profound loss. Her parents were alive and well and living out their dream of self-sufficiency on ten acres of land west of Missoula. "Harlan, as your attorney, I should stick to legal matters but, in this case, I'm going to make an exception. Get therapy—both of you." She slid a business card across the desk. "Here's the number of a counselor who comes highly recommended."

Jason shook his head.

She wasn't ready to admit defeat. "What would your mom say if you killed someone?"

The teen looked at his hands as his chin wobbled.

"You both need to talk to a therapist. I suggest you look at this as an opportunity to get your life on track."

Ten minutes later, Sophia watched them from her office window. Jason's head hung as his father urged him into their new model Mercedes. All the money in the world couldn't stop an eighteen year old from missing his mother.

Given their situation, she would've taken the case for free, but the Squints were wealthy people and could easily afford her services. Their check would go into her pro bono fund, which was the heart and soul of her work as a defense lawyer. To make a real difference, she wanted to represent people who wouldn't be able to afford an attorney of her ability. The money would help pay for scientific testing, specialized experts, or hiring a private investigator. Every extra penny she earned went into an account to help the wrongly accused.

"You took advantage." Detective Mateo Ramirez of the Granite City-Elkhead County police department stood in the doorway of her office. He was dressed in a crisp white shirt and a gray tie that matched his gray dress pants. His short-cropped black hair was, as always, perfectly combed. He was the sexiest man she had ever encountered. She wished he were an idiot, the type of man who was pretty but had the brain of a gnat. Unfortunately, he was also the most intelligent detective in the department. The man was a stud with a capitol *S*.

She fluttered her eyelashes, playing dumb just to annoy him, as she relaxed into her office chair. "I did?"

"You knew Detective Needham mixed up the cases, and you said nothing." He slammed her office door shut and then marched to her desk, his movement's fluid and smooth. It was like watching Michelangelo's *David* in motion. She itched to touch his warm skin and feel the rush of desire when his clever hands reciprocated but contained her response. They had ended their relationship twelve years ago because of irreconcilable differences, and nothing in their recent history suggested they could get along.

"I don't know what you're talking about." He was obviously referring to Jason Squint, but baiting him was too much fun to resist.

He stalked around her desk, his steps stiff and controlled as though he was forcing himself to slow down. He stopped and placed his hands on either side of her office chair, trapping her.

She should be scared, but instead she was exhilarated. This was Mateo. As much as she worked to irritate him, she knew he would never hurt her. He just didn't like her. Any affection he'd had for her had disappeared, replaced by obvious disapproval.

That was fine with her. She felt nothing but disdain and resentment for him, so she figured they were even on that score. It gave her unending joy to defeat him on the stand or beat him at their little game of who could antagonize whom the most.

And yet a small traitorous part of her still yearned for him. Especially when she saw fire in his dark eyes, smelt his musky aftershave, or watched him move with a grace and economy that took her breath away.

****

Heat coursed through Mateo's veins as it always

did whenever she was around. Her large, luminous green eyes, her upturned nose, and her smooth skin always disturbed him, throwing him off balance. He reined in his physical reaction. She was one of the most gifted lawyers he had ever encountered and could have had a career with any prosecuting attorney's office. But no, she had to practice as a defense attorney. It wasn't logical, but it felt like she had betrayed him. It was as though she had gone out of her way to hurt him.

"You should've told Needham he'd mixed up the cases."

She stared at him as though he'd lost his mind. "That's crazy. It's not my job to do his thinking for him." She rocked back in her chair.

He either had to release his hold on the armrests or end up in her lap. He chose to stand.

She placed her feet on her desk. The action made her skirt slip up her thighs, revealing the top of her stockings.

He imagined running his hand over her pale, silky flesh. Back in the day, she'd had the sexiest underwear collection, and from the look of things, that hadn't changed. Blood surged to his penis. He thumped the desk, burying his unwelcome attraction. "Bullshit. You have a responsibility—"

"No. I have a responsibility to my client." Her smug look told him she felt no remorse for letting a dangerous kid back onto the streets.

"You should at least have—"

"If you cared that much about the case, you

should have gone to court yourself." She crossed her ankles. Was it an intentional attempt to distract him? Maybe make him remember what it felt like to have her long, luscious legs wrapped around his waist.

She gave him a knowing smile. She was playing with him. She knew he had a physical weakness for her and was using it to confuse him.

He shook his head, denying not only her charge, but also his own emotional turmoil. "It wasn't my —"

"Bull." She sat up straighter in her chair. Her skirt hitched farther up her legs. "You were off duty when you came upon the scene."

"We stopped to help a fellow officer." He glanced at her breasts. Her nipples pressed against a plain white blouse that wasn't sexy or revealing in any way, yet was somehow more enticing than her lace stockings. He licked his dry lips. He had to keep his mind on the case. "There's nothing wrong with that?"

"Right, but why is your partner testifying in a case that clearly belongs to the patrolling officer?"

He bent over her, closing the short distance between them so they were inches apart. "The kid was drunk."

She lifted her chin, meeting his gaze, not backing down. "He'd just lost his mother. Where's your compassion?"

His nose was almost touching hers. "Where's your compassion for the woman whose house he wrecked when he swerved off the road and drove into it?"

"She has house insurance and she can sue. No one was hurt."

"What about next time?" He was very aware of her scent, honey mixed with apples. God, he wanted to taste her.

"There won't be a next time." She snapped out the words like a volley from a rifle.

"You have an answer for everything. If I had any sense, I would shut you up," he replied in the same tone. Her body, her mouth, even his own anger, were getting to him. He should back away, but he couldn't.

"I dare you," she whispered, her lips almost touching his.

He kissed her. She was the most frustrating, dangerous, sexy woman he had ever met. And she was kissing him back. Her hands wrapped around his neck, tugging him down, deepening the kiss as her tongue dipped into his mouth. How had he lived without her, without this, for so long?

He placed his hands around her waist and hoisted her out of the chair, aligning their bodies, pressing his erect penis against the apex of her thighs.

She moaned and wrapped her legs around him as she rotated her pelvis, driving him out of control. He explored her mouth with his tongue. He ran his hands over the soft flesh of her upper thighs, then her butt, and up to her breasts, frantic to touch every inch of her. Everything was familiar, but at the same time new and exciting. He sat her on the desk and broke the kiss.

When she looked up at him, her eyes were glazed with passion. He was lost. It was as if all their resentment and anger about their past had coalesced into this one charged moment. And their sexual desire that they had both buried would no longer stay hidden.

He reached under her skirt and tore off her panties. At the same time, she unzipped his fly and pushed his underwear down, releasing him.

He should slow down and make sure she was ready. He didn't want to hurt her. But she grabbed his cock and wiggled forward so he rested against the entrance to her vagina.

He groaned. She had told him without words exactly what she wanted. With one hard thrust, he was in her up to the hilt. She was warm and moist. Every muscle, every fiber of his being, was energized, as if he'd just plugged his dick into an electrical outlet.

He lifted her up so she was completely impaled on him. She threw her head back and sighed as he slid deeper.

He stepped back and dropped down into the office chair.

She rotated her hips again, easing herself up until only his tip was still inside her, and then she slid down, taking every last inch of him.

Oh, god. The sensation of her rising and falling propelled him closer to the edge. He wasn't going to last. She had him by the balls...literally.

He tore open her blouse. He wanted to touch her breasts, feel their weight, and enjoy her velvety skin. He recalled how much it excited her when he played with them. It was as though there was an invisible string that ran from her chest to her clitoris. All he had to do was strum it.

He slipped her bra cups down and pushed the straps aside. He wet his lips at the sight of her small, round, perfectly pink areolas.

She stopped, her breath coming in loud gasps. Her hair flopped over her face. He thought about brushing it aside, but flicked her nipple instead.

The muscles of her inner wall clamped around his penis. He bit out a curse and then sucked her breast into his mouth.

She moved then, pounding onto him. Hard and fast. He grabbed her hips, setting the tempo. He couldn't stop and didn't want to.

She screamed as her orgasm hit and then he joined her, giving himself over to the overwhelming lust that only Sophia could awaken within him.

****

Sophia eased herself up and off Mateo's lap. She refused to look at his spent penis. His sperm dribbled down her leg. *Oh, god.* She hadn't even been smart enough to use a condom.

She wiggled her skirt down, tugged up her bra, and then clasped her shirt closed covering her breasts. Her hands were shaking so much she couldn't manage the buttons. What was she thinking? She hadn't been thinking, and that was the problem.

She turned and headed for her private bathroom, not making eye contact. If he had a smug look on his face, she might kill him, and that was something she would regret, even more than the sexual encounter.

"You can see yourself out," she said as she closed the door, and was amazed at how calm and distant she sounded.

She stared at herself in the mirror. Her skin was flushed from her neck up, her hair was in disarray, and she had the wild-eyed look of someone who had done something incredibly stupid.

She would've liked a shower, but her bathroom was small with just a sink and a toilet. She waited until she heard him leave and then grabbed a handful of toilet paper and cleaned herself as best she could.

Why was she so vulnerable to him? It was obvious he didn't like her. Maybe it was like muscle memory... Yeah right...sex muscle memory.

She washed her hands and then splashed some water on her face.

She'd met him twelve years ago at the University of Montana when they'd attended a course about the philosophy of law. The program was dry and boring. The most exciting thing about the class was seeing Mateo. By the end of the semester, he asked her out. She'd ended up in his bed on their first date, and they had spent the weekend together. They'd lain entwined in each other's arms, shared showers, and made love a dozen times.

After that, they had been inseparable until the end of the school year when he attended the police academy and she went to law school. One evening they were sitting in their favorite fast food joint when he brought up the subject of their future. He'd imagined her working for the U.S. Attorney's Office for the District of Montana. She'd had to set him straight. She'd always wanted to be a defense attorney, and nothing he said was going to change her goal.

She'd tried to explain her reason for her career choice, but he refused to listen. No matter how much they argued, she couldn't make him understand that the justice system only worked when the accused was allowed a free and fair trial. Even worse, he couldn't forgive her for not agreeing with him. She had been in love with him, but he obviously hadn't loved her in return. If he had he would've found a way to live with her career choice as a defense lawyer. Instead, he had stormed out leaving her sitting in the restaurant with a cold burger and a flat coke.

That was the last time she'd seen him until two years ago when she had the opportunity of a partnership with a law firm in Granite City.

Since the moment he had spotted her in court, he had been dismissive. Every look, every word, seemed to drip with disdain. Not that she had allowed his obvious contempt to bother her. She countered with her own brand of remote disapproval. If she thought a quirk of her lips, a glare, or an argument would annoy him, then she gleefully employed it. But she had never intended for it to lead to sex.

She didn't know how things would be between them now, but it would never lead to anything. He saw her as the enemy, and she hated him for it.

CHAPTER TWO

Mateo took a last sip of his coffee as he marched across the Granite City Square toward the law courts. He needed to talk to Sophia Reed. He'd lain awake half the night thinking about their encounter. He was shocked by his own actions. He'd always been vulnerable to her. How could he not, when she was still as smart and beautiful now as she had been all those years ago? He'd gone to her office to talk to her, but the moment he'd laid eyes on her, he'd lost his temper. That reaction had cracked through his self-discipline and allowed his unwanted attraction to surface. He'd let himself be seduced by her bewitching green eyes, fantastic body, and her intoxicating scent. She'd short-circuited his brain. Even now, as angry as he was at his own weakness, just thinking about her made his penis twitch.

He'd witnessed her in court on numerous occasions. Cops practiced their testimony if they were to be questioned by her. She wasn't bombastic or rude like some of her colleagues. She was sweet, intelligent, articulate, and could spot a lie from a hundred feet away. And she always went in for the kill. His department had lost too many cases because she had managed to prove reasonable doubt.

She was right about Needham. The man was barely tolerable as a partner. He was arrogant, reckless, sloppy, and an idiot. That was a dangerous combination. Mateo only hoped that given enough rope, he would hang himself, especially if he underestimated Sophia in the courtroom.

On the outside, she was plain with fine pale brown hair that always seemed a little messy, yet was so soft he itched to caress it. Her clothes never fit right. Her sleeves were too long and her jackets were always on the large side. But underneath the ill-fitting pantsuits and messy hair, she was a firecracker. He wanted nothing more than to bury himself in her over and over again until...

Damn it, he needed some self-control.

Perhaps last night didn't matter to her. There were people who could compartmentalize their feelings, although the Sophia he'd known twelve years ago wasn't like that. There had been a time when he'd been careless in his sexual encounters, but not anymore. He'd matured, had relationships, been married and divorced. He knew the difference between love and lust. With Sophia, the lust was off the scale; it always had been. They'd dated for about six months when they were in university. That was before he'd discovered her plan to become Montana's leading defense attorney.

They'd seen each other in court a number of times, and she'd hardly acknowledged him. She simply gave him a slight nod of the head and then continued about her business as though he meant nothing. Although, he had to admit he was partly responsible for their coolness. He hadn't gone out of his way to be friendly with her. He was a cop, and she was a DA. He put bad guys away and she got them off. Their differences in ideologies were too wide to span. As far as he was concerned, she was the opposition. Her choice of career felt like a betrayal of everything he had worked to achieve. Yet there was something about her... A sweetness that had grabbed him and wouldn't let go.

Last night when they were alone, he'd sensed her vulnerability, as seductive as she was with her mind-blowing legs, exceptional breasts, and sexy lingerie. When he'd seen the passion in her eyes, it was like being hit in the stomach with a crowbar. She disturbed him on an emotional level, and he didn't like it one bit.

He hadn't gone to her office for sex, or to argue. He'd wanted to ask her to defend an innocent teenager who was accused of arson. Now he had to hunt her down at the courthouse because the kid was still in trouble.

Perhaps it would be better if he spoke to her on the street in public. It was a risk. He didn't want anyone in the department to hear. Not that he was doing anything illicit, but his colleagues on the force wouldn't appreciate him acquiring legal aid for a suspect. But he'd never sent an innocent to jail, and he wasn't about to start now.

He just hoped Sophia would agree to work for free because there was no way he could afford to pay her exorbitant fees.

He spotted her running down the wide, stone steps of the courthouse. She was wearing a brown pantsuit, a white blouse, and a pair of flat, black pumps. The pants were okay, but the jacket was way too big. It was as if she was trying to hide her body, and maybe she was. A lot of creeps went through the court system. There was no way any sane woman would want to attract their attention. He pushed the thought aside as he quickened his pace so he could intercept her. This time they would talk without the distraction of sex.

**

Sophia groaned when she spotted Mateo making a beeline for her. She was tempted to turn around and run back inside, but she didn't want him to read her actions as a sign of weakness.

Once again, he wore a gray tie, dark gray pants, and a white dress shirt with the sleeves rolled halfway up his arms. His police issue gun and badge were attached to his belt at his waist. She couldn't decide if the clothes made him look sexy or if he would be just as hot without them. That thought made her imagine him naked. Her hands tingled with the need to touch him as her nipples hardened. She looked to the clear blue sky, praying she could control her physical response. It was an unwanted reminder of just how susceptible she was to him.

He halted in front of her, blocking her path. "I need to talk to you."

She sidestepped, dodging around him, without

making eye contact. "I can't stop. I'm late."

That was true as far as it went. She needed to get to the bank before it closed for the weekend. There were bills due, and if she didn't deposit the check from Harlen Squint into her pro bono fund, she wouldn't be able to pay them.

He grabbed her elbow, spinning her around, forcing her to look at him. "This isn't about last night. It's about a kid. He needs your help."

She looked at the ground as she thought about the ramifications of his words. He needed her services as an attorney. She raised her burgundy leather briefcase, holding it in front of herself like a shield. Not that it could protect her from anything, especially her own traitorous body, but it made her feel a little more secure. She schooled her features, refusing to let him see her self-doubt and hesitancy.

"Why should I help you?" She hated how defensive she sounded.

"You won't be helping me. You'd be stopping an innocent fifteen year old from going to jail. Do all your defendants need large bank accounts before you'll help them?" He curled his lip into a sneer.

She stamped her foot and poked him in the chest. "Do you think your disgust matters to me? I neither need nor want your approval, but for the record, more than half my clients are pro bono."

He sucked in a deep breath and held up his hands in a show of surrender, obviously realizing if he wanted her help, he had to be at least civil to her. An inked rose peeked out of the shirtsleeve on his right arm. She hadn't noticed his tattoo last night. She'd been busy, preoccupied with sex, and he hadn't taken off his shirt. Did he have other tattoos? She dismissed the thought, knowing she needed her wits about her when dealing with him, and she couldn't allow herself to be distracted by his physique.

"I apologize." He rubbed his temple as though he had a headache forming. "Look, this is about a kid's life. All I'm asking is that you listen."

"You'll have to walk with me. As I said, I'm late." She sprinted past him, expecting him to follow.

He easily matched her stride. "There's this kid. He's a snotty little jackass."

She gave him what she hoped was a withering look. "Which translates to mean he's making your job hard and won't admit to a crime he probably didn't commit."

"That's not… He's not telling us the whole truth about what he was doing—"

"What are the charges?" She cut him off, needing to get to the heart of the matter as quickly as possible. The sooner he explained, the sooner he could be on his way.

"Arson, causing deliberate homicide."

"That's a hefty indictment, one which carries a minimum sentence of ten years. Luckily, as a minor, he can avoid a death penalty."

A bead of sweat appeared on Mateo's forehead as he kept pace. "As I said, I don't think he did it, but if detective Needham has his way, Ty Washburn will go down." He met her gaze, seeming earnest and serious. His whole focus appeared to be on the accused. Last night hadn't affected him at all.

She would always be at a disadvantage where their relationship was concerned. That was just the way it was. He could have her over a barrel, under a table, standing, sitting…any way he wanted. It was only a small sense of survival that warned her to keep her distance.

She was almost sprinting now as her body echoed her emotions. She wanted to get the information out of Mateo as fast as possible and send him on his way, but getting heatstroke because she was running in the late August sun wasn't going to achieve anything. A tickle of perspiration dribbled down her back, and she slowed her pace.

Once again, he matched her stride. She was pleased to see sweat stains had formed on his perfectly pressed white shirt. "Detective Needham is convinced that Ty set fire to his apartment complex. Two people died in the blaze."

"What sort of case does he have?"

"The kid was seen arguing with the landlord, and the fire started in his family's storage locker."

"Is that all?"

"The building in question is a dump. It's also in a part of town where property prices are going up."

"And you think the landlord could easily have set the fire and hidden the materials in the locker."

They had reached the bank. He stepped ahead of her and opened the door. "The landlord has an alibi, and there's no evidence to prove he did it, but he could've hired someone. It isn't rocket science."

He followed her into the cool interior. The bank was an old building that dated back to the beginning of the twentieth century with white granite walls that seemed to deflect the summer heat.

She stopped, waiting for her eyes to adjust. There were very few windows, which meant the gloom inside was a stark contrast to the late afternoon sun.

She nodded at the young receptionist, who sat at her desk near the entrance, and then hurried to join the lineup that was marked off by ropes attached to short free-standing poles.

The spacious lobby was tastefully decorated in cherry-stained paneling. It also boasted a highly polished hardwood floor. The whole place reflected the opulence of a bygone era.

Mateo stood next to her. His musky aftershave combined with his natural odor made her heart beat faster.

She buttoned her jacket, hoping it would provide her with another layer of protection against him.

His dark gaze snagged hers. "I need to know if you're going to take the case."

CHAPTER THREE

Of course, she would help Ty Washburn. The real problem was Mateo. The fact he had sought her out to help an innocent reminded her why she had fallen in love with him all those years ago. Above all things, he was a man of integrity, and in her experience, that was a quality in short supply. Would taking this case put her in close proximity to him? Was that something she wanted?

The disturbance Mateo caused within her was like a thunderstorm. One part was the heat of sex and the other the cool distance of their interactions. When they clashed, there would be nothing but trouble. The whole situation left her feeling off-balance, and she wasn't sure how much she could take.

She observed the other patrons, giving herself time to consider the best course of action. There were ten people ahead in the lineup. They all appeared to be focused on the three staff members, intently waiting their turn. All accept for one white-haired person who stood off to the side, filling out a form. Sophia couldn't tell if it was a man or a woman. They wore unisex sweatpants and sweatshirt. The longer white hair suggested a woman, but their square shape seemed to be that of a male. Sophia shook her head. It didn't matter who the patrons were, and how they were dressed was none of her business.

A short, solid middle-aged man in a wrinkled suit left his corner office and headed for the front door, keys in hand. Sophia assumed he was the manager planning to lock the doors.

There had never been any doubt she would take the case. She'd only hesitated because of Mateo. But that probably wouldn't be an issue. He would want to distance himself from her and the indictment so as not to appear conflicted.

She turned to him. "I will help this child because..."

He ignored her, watching the entrance. He didn't even blink. He seemed to be fascinated by the manager at the door.

Two men marched into the bank, each of them carrying a large black tote. Both were dressed in dark clothing and wearing rubber masks. One was disguised as an old man, the other a baby. They thrust the manager aside. He hit the wall on the right, throwing his glasses askew.

Mateo shoved her down and away from him.

She instinctively put her hands out to protect herself, dropping her briefcase as she fell to her knees.

Mateo aimed his handgun at the two men who were in the process of tugging large guns from their totes.

"Police, put your weapons down." Mateo's voice was loud and forceful.

Someone grabbed her arm and yanked her to her feet. She tried to turn to see her assailant but he shoved a hard, metal object against her temple. She froze, not daring to move.

"Drop the gun, hero, or I'll shoot the woman," a man's voice shouted in her ear.

She winced. This couldn't be happening. One minute she'd been arguing with Mateo, and the next someone was holding a firearm to her head.

Mateo cut his gaze in her direction as he aimed his weapon at the two would-be robbers near the entrance. He seemed controlled, confident, falling back on his police training.

She tried to struggle against her attacker, but he held tight, jerking her back against his chest, trapping her in a vice-like grip.

He aimed the gun at Mateo. "Stop moving or do you want me to put a bullet in your boyfriend? His breath warmed her ear when he spoke. The stench of his body odor mixed with the smell of rubber made a nauseating concoction. It took all her willpower not to gag.

She heeded his warning and stilled, trying not to flinch, and resisted the urge to pull away. She didn't want Mateo to die because of her.

Once she quit fighting, her captor put the barrel against her head. "Do you want a dead girlfriend?" he snarled at Mateo.

Mateo held one hand up in surrender as he

lowered his pistol to the ground.

Sophia's heart thudded in her chest as she stared at the firearm lying on the floor. He wouldn't have yielded his weapon if there was a possibility of getting out of this situation. That meant he had assessed their chances and considered it hopeless.

"Smart choice." The gunman propelled Sophia toward Mateo, who caught her and protectively tucked her close to his side.

She straightened away from him, not because she didn't want the comfort of his embrace, but because she didn't want to hamper him. He might have to move fast to defend himself or the bank customers, and she refused to be in the way.

The man who had threatened her wore a latex mask depicting an elderly woman, complete with a full head of white hair. It fitted his face perfectly and moved with his gestures. When he talked, the lips responded, as did the eyes and the cheeks. It had to be glued on. This wasn't a cheap costume. This was a top-of-the-line Hollywood-quality product that looked real. Who were these guys that they could afford the kind of disguise that ran into the hundreds, if not thousands, of dollars?

He was the unisex person who'd been filling out forms in the lobby. The masked man had been waiting for his cohorts to arrive. He'd been prepared and ready.

He positioned himself behind them. "I can shoot either of you in a second so don't get any ideas.

The thief who posed as a baby shoved the manager toward the front door, forcing him to lock it. He and the robber who masqueraded as an old man, wore cheaper disguises, their features distorted into terrifying caricatures.

Baby gave a high-pitched hoot. "The bank is now closed for the weekend."

Ice trickled down Sophia's spine. They were trapped.

Old Man waved his weapon at the lineup of customers. "I want everyone to stand in the middle of the lobby." He pointed his gun at the tellers. "You, too. All of you toss your phones onto the floor."

One by one, the customers and staff navigated the roped barriers and moved to the wide-open space in the middle of the foyer, throwing their devices in a neat pile on the way. They all had the same wide-eyed, blanched expression of disbelief.

Sophia stepped forward, ready to join the others.

"Not you." Old Woman still stood behind them, weapon aimed at their heads. "You two stay where you are." He raised his voice. "This is a bank robbery. We're going to be here for a while. You will be tied. Do not resist. This is for your own safety. If you obey our instructions, you will be released unharmed."

Old Man dug inside his tote bag and extracted a bundle of long black plastic strips. Baby stood near the exit, aiming his gun at the hostages. He seemed calm and focused. Sophia had no doubt he would shoot if necessary.

Fifteen people crowded together in the center of the room. The group was mainly male. There were only four women including her. Two of them had gray hair, one a customer and one a cashier. The other young woman, the receptionist, had long brown hair and looked to be in her mid-twenties. She couldn't stop crying. Her trembling hands and pale face, along with her quiet sobbing, revealed her tangible fear.

The rest of the detainees represented a large slice of society. One gentleman looked quite elderly, and it took him a while to walk to the middle of the room. Six of the group were wearing overalls and most likely did some kind of manual labor. The rest, including the bank manager, wore business suits. Their shocked expressions reflected the trauma they undoubtedly felt.

Old Woman continued to shout orders. "Baby, keep an eye out for the police. Old Man, search the cop and his girlfriend. Pat them down. They probably have other weapons and then use the zip ties. After they're secure, do the same with the others."

Old Man's hands traveled along Mateo's arms and then his torso. When he reached Mateo's right ankle, he stopped and tugged up his pant leg to reveal a combat knife.

While Old Man and Old Woman were occupied with Mateo, Sophia pushed her smartwatch as far up her wrist as it would go. She tried to make her movements small and slow so they wouldn't attract any attention. Then she tugged the sleeve of her jacket down so it covered most of her hand.

Old Man secured Mateo's wrists and pointed to

the wall underneath the teller windows "Sit."

Mateo complied, taking one knee first, and then rolling to a seated position on the ground. He made it look easy but Sophia doubted she'd be able duplicate the feat without falling flat on her face.

Old Man stood in front of her. Although his mask covered his face, she could see his eyes. He leered, and she imagined him licking his lips. She turned away as bile rose in her throat. He grabbed her breasts, kneading them.

"No." She stepped back, batting his hands away.

Old Woman nudged Old man with his gun. "Cut that out. If you hurt her, I will kill you."

Old Man recoiled as if he'd been slapped, holding his hands in the air. "I was just playing around. Besides, I've always wanted to take a cop."

"She's not a cop. She's a defense attorney," Mateo shouted from across the room. "You should treat her with respect. You're gonna need her when this is over."

"A defense attorney, huh?" Old Woman snagged her briefcase from the floor and rifled through her belongings until he found her ID. "It says here you're Sophia Reed and you're a member of the Bar Association."

Sophia held her breath as Old Man continued his body check without molesting her. His hands were shaking as he groped her arms. He stopped at her elbows so he missed her watch.

Old Man had just finished binding Sophia's wrists when Old Woman said, "Keep her and the cop together. They could come in handy."

Old Man shoved Sophia toward the teller windows where Mateo sat. She eased herself down to one knee just as Mateo had earlier and then tipped to the side and fell on her butt. It wasn't graceful, but it got the job done.

Mateo shifted closer so his shoulder touched hers. He smiled and winked at her, providing her some much needed assurance.

Old Woman walked to the center of the lobby. "Which one of you is the bank manager?"

The same portly man who had locked the front door raised a quivering hand. Old Woman led him behind the teller's windows and then along a hallway to the right, presumably to open the safe.

At the same time, Old man methodically worked his way through the hostages. It seemed to take hours, but the robbers didn't appear to be in a hurry. Old Man was thorough and efficient which, for some reason, Sophia found creepy. The masks, the guns, and the palpable fear of the victims made the whole thing seem like a bizarre Halloween party that had gone terribly wrong.

Mateo leaned back against the wall. "We might as well relax a little and save our energy."

His confidence didn't seem feigned. And the fact he was able to take their situation in stride irritated her. Violent men who had already threatened to kill them were holding them captive. She wanted to argue with him. If only because arguing would make her feel more in control than just sitting here waiting, but she knew he was right.

She leant against the dark, rich wood molding that covered the lower half of the partition. It was not as comfortable as he made it appear. She couldn't find a position where her spine wasn't overextended because her hands were secured behind her and in the way. She fidgeted from one side to the other. Finally, she rested on her left side, facing Mateo, with her shoulder against the wall.

Old Man pulled three small plastic bundles from his tote and unfolded them, revealing full-size backpacks. He busied himself emptying the cash drawers and stuffing the money into the packs. He hauled everything into the vault area out of sight.

A few minutes later he returned, escorting the manager back to the lobby. He double-checked the front door, making sure it was locked, and then nodded to Baby. "I'll be in the back with the boss. Call when the cops arrive."

Baby gave him a thumbs up. "Affirmative."

Sophia breathed a sigh of relief at his departure. For her, Old Man was the scariest criminal because of the sickening interest he had shown in her.

She jumped as the sound of banging rang through the bank. "Do you think they're raiding the safety deposit boxes?" she whispered. It was a stupid question because this was a robbery. Why would they go to all this trouble if they weren't going to take all the valuables?

Mateo's lips grazed her ear. It was strange how comforting she found his touch, his scent, and his familiarity, when less than an hour ago she had been upset with him.

"Thank God, this bank doesn't have a security guard."

"I thought that would be a deterrent."

"No, statistics from the FBI show that when armed guards are present during robberies, violence escalates."

"Is that why you relinquished your gun?"

"Yes, I should have never drawn my weapon in the first place. I guess it was instinct. Then I realized I was outgunned and that my actions were placing everyone in danger. Plus, this is different from most bank heists," he murmured.

"How?"

"Normally, the perpetrators walk in, hand a note to the teller, and then walk out with whatever is in the cash drawer. They rarely result in hostage situations. These guys planned to take prisoners." He looked at the ceiling. "Although I'm surprised they haven't done anything to take out the cameras, and I'm not sure they really want the cash from the vault."

"They just took the manager back there. We can hear them smashing things. Of course, they want the money."

He tried to shrug, but could only move one shoulder. "Maybe, but how much are we talking about? People don't carry that much cash anymore. Most of us use plastic, so how much could be in there? Fifty grand? A hundred? Maybe more, but probably less than a million. I think they want whatever is in the safety deposit boxes. Which brings up some other questions."

"Like what?"

"The contents are left in secret. No one knows what's in them, not even the bank staff. Police raids on banks in Spain and England have produced stolen art, illegal weapons, and in one case here in the States they found fake identities."

"What's your point?"

"How do they know there's anything in there worth taking?"

"Maybe they have a connection to the people who rent the boxes."

"Exactly." He frowned. "Breaking into them takes time and so does a hostage negotiation. I'll bet one of the tellers pressed the alarm under their desk, which is probably what they want. I don't have a view of the street from here. Do you?"

She arched her neck. The only window she could see was above the solid oak front door. It was just a thin strip of glass. The rest of the natural light came from skylights in the ceiling. "No."

"An officer has probably driven by. They might have even checked the doors."

"Which are locked. What's their next move?"

"Make contact. The police will need to call and make sure it's not a false alarm.

At that moment, the phone rang.

CHAPTER FOUR

The phone had been ringing on and off for three hours, but the assholes hadn't answered it. Mateo was convinced the bastards were stalling. Sirens wailed in the distance and then fell silent as they neared. The bright afternoon light had given way to dusk, and the strobe lights from the emergency vehicles reflected through the skylights.

He closed his eyes, trying to envision what was happening outside. The Granite City-Elkhead County Police had probably secured the area. They would also be assembling the SWAT team. He had no doubt that, given enough time with no communication, the highly trained tactical unit would storm the building. The question was, how long would it take?

He needed to form a plan and help free the hostages, but there was very little he could do. He was unarmed and cuffed, leaving him all but useless. Hopefully an opportunity would arise that would allow him to protect the captives. But that didn't seem likely since the robbers had ignored the phone, refusing to negotiate. The only thing that would help the police at this point was tactical information. Unfortunately, he had no way of contacting them. All he could do was wait.

Sophia fidgeted beside him. "You're a jerk." She kept her voice low so as not to attract attention.

He matched her tone. "So I've been told, but why do you think so?"

She met his gaze, giving him a long pained look and then broke eye contact. "Being with you was a mistake."

She hadn't answered his question, but he let it go. "You mean twelve years ago or yesterday?"

"I was talking about our pheromone-induced relationship twelve years ago." She wrinkled her pert little nose, suggesting he was just playing dumb. She wasn't wrong. He didn't want to talk about why they'd split up, especially while they were being held hostage. So far, she had shown remarkable strength of character. Most people would be too shook up to form a sentence let alone start in on their ex. He remembered her pulling away from him when he'd tried to protect her at the outset of the robbery. He couldn't be sure, but he suspected she hadn't wanted him to put himself between her and the scumbags. That was unexpected, and spoke not only to her independence but also her bravery.

"I enjoy the pheromone-induced thing." He grinned, knowing his answer would annoy her, but why he felt the need to antagonize her he couldn't say.

She shifted her gaze to the hardwood floor, her expression unreadable. "Forget it, and forget about last night, too."

"Do you blame me for that?" She should. He was the one who had slammed into her office. He had started it, which was something he, surprisingly, didn't regret.

"No, I'm mad at myself. I don't know what I was thinking. I'm not the kind of woman who can jump into bed with a man and not get emotionally involved."

He studied her, trying to figure out what was going on, but mind-reading had never been his specialty. He was able to sift through detailed evidence and bombard suspects with perceptive questions. Then he would read their body language and know when they were lying. But he was deaf and blind when it came to his personal relationships. He had never ended an affair on good terms. It had always gotten ugly. "My ex-wife called me a jerk on steroids, which was a bit harsh considering she cheated on me."

"You were married?"

"Not for long. It ended five years ago. I always blamed her." Perhaps it was time to own up to his part in their separation. "To be honest, I'm not great at dividing my time. I get so caught up in a case, I can't seem to think about anything else. I guess I neglected her."

"You are very focused. Did you go to marriage counseling?"

"She never suggested it. I don't think either of us wanted to do the work." Sometime in the future, he wanted a family. What if he was unable to learn from his mistakes? Or worse, couldn't let work go once he left the precinct?

"It's the silence that breaks the bond." She spoke as though she understood, and maybe she did.

He wondered if she had ever been married or had a long-term boyfriend. "What's your story?"

"I went out with this guy for three years. In the end, we split up and I moved to Granite City."

"No acrimony."

She gave a low chuckle. It was a harsh sound, full of bitterness. "He said I emasculated him. My success as an attorney reflected poorly on him, and he couldn't bear to be around me."

"Did he have a name?"

"Robert...Rob."

"Here's what you need to do. Imagine you're standing in front of good ol' Rob. Now bend your knee and give him a good swift kick in the balls. Don't worry. He's not a man so he won't need them. Only weak men are threatened by strong women. I see it all the time. I think Rob did you a favor by leaving."

She giggled, the sound warming his insides, making him realize how much he wanted to see her outside of work. Last night, they had savored each other physically, but he didn't know anything of her life now. He really wanted to tease her and hear her laugh, and he didn't want to wait another twelve years to do it. "Where do we go from here?"

She stared at the ceiling, taking a moment, and then faced him. "I thought we could carry on as though we don't know each other. You know, like we do now."

"You want to ignore me?"

She glared at him, her eyes dark green in the fading twilight. "Isn't that what you've been doing for the last two years?"

He was genuinely taken aback. He'd considered their relationship professional. It had never occurred to him that he was snubbing her. "I'm sorry. I didn't realize."

She snorted. "Bull."

"No, it's not—"

"You look the other way when you see me coming."

"I do not."

"Yes, you do, and if our paths cross and you can't avoid me, you just give me a vague nod. You're so embarrassed to be seen with me, you can't even say hello." She raised her voice. "Look at how you were in the Timothy Morgan case."

The robber with the baby mask hadn't paid them any attention, and he wanted to keep it that way. He pursed his lips, meaning to put a finger to them, but couldn't with his hands tied behind his back. "Hush. This isn't the place to have this conversation."

"Why, do you have anything better to do? We're stuck here for the duration so I might as well tell you that you are a selfish, egotistical, stuck up, SOB fart-brain."

Her words hit him like a punch to the gut. His ex-wife liked to reel off a whole string of names, but they had never been great together. Her spite hadn't bothered him. They'd drifted into marriage the way people do when they've been dating for a while and need to liven up their relationship. Sophia's anger hurt.

He shifted so he was no longer leaning on his shoulder, facing her. Instead, he rested the back of his head against the wall, taking the time to sort through everything she had said. As far as he was concerned, she was off base. He was all business when their paths crossed on a case, and there was nothing wrong with that.

Finally, he turned toward her, once again leaning on his side. "I don't understand why you're so mad about the way we greet each other."

Her eyes widened, and then she made a face that suggested he'd lost his mind. "You have to be kidding me."

"No. I'm civil to you. I'm just not friendly towards you, and do you know why?" He didn't give her time to answer. "Because I'm a cop and you're a defense attorney, which is exactly why we broke up in the first place. You could work for any prosecutor's office in the state."

"This again. I am as much a part of the justice—"

"I work damn hard to find the bad guys, get the evidence against them, and I obey the law while I'm doing it. Then people like you stand up for them in court and get them off on a technicality."

She shook her head. Soft brown strands of hair fell in her face. "Four."

"What do you mean 'four'?"

"I've negotiated tons of cases and won the majority of them, but there are only four judgments that really matter. In each case, I worked pro bono and proved my clients innocent. Those men would've ended up in jail if I hadn't worked like a dog for them. We have due process in this country. That means you can't just point the finger at someone and say, 'You're guilty.' You have to prove it. We do not live in a dictatorship. Maybe we're on different sides of the justice equation, but we both play an important part."

He nodded and opened his mouth to speak, but she beat him to it. "Most criminals plead guilty in the face of overwhelming evidence. If they walk free, then you didn't do your job very well."

There was something in the rigidity of her body. Maybe she was just stressed over their situation. They were bound hostages caught up in a bank robbery. The robbers were crashing through the vault, presumably ransacking the safety deposits. But the pain in her eyes, the way she pressed her lips together, and the tension in her spine told him there was more to her story. "Why did you become a lawyer?"

She turned away.

"You might as well tell me. We don't have anything better to do," he said, throwing her words back at her.

The other hostages sat quietly in the center of the room. An older woman comforted the still sobbing receptionist, who couldn't seem to control her fear. The manager had glared at her several times, as had some of the others, but their irritation wouldn't make any difference to her blind terror.

Sophia gave him a cool look, which suggested he was a slug. "I'll tell you, but you have to give me your word you won't tell any of your cop friends."

"Okaaaay." He drew out the word, wondering what she could possibly have to hide.

"When I was fifteen, my father was accused of manslaughter. His car killed a pedestrian. He wasn't driving, but the vehicle was damaged, and he couldn't prove it wasn't him at the wheel. He was arrested, denied bail, and sent to jail. My mom and I went to live with my Aunt Valerie. Mom sold our house and spent every penny we had on lawyers. In the end, she found a good one. He managed to prove Dad's innocence. Our neighbor's son had 'borrowed' the car. A red-light camera had taken his picture. I do this job for all the men and women who are wrongly accused. Everyone is entitled to their day in court."

Why hadn't she told him this twelve years ago? The pain she'd endured at having her innocent father go to jail was still with her today. Her life had been shattered, and she'd undergone the nightmare of having her world ripped apart. These were the circumstances that had shaped her into the driven attorney she was today.

The detectives on the case had to have known about the red-light camera. Had they been lazy or just hadn't wanted to admit they were wrong? Sophia was strong, independent, and prepared to fight to ensure the system worked. It surprised him to realize he respected her.

She fidgeted and attempted to roll her shoulders. The action made her jacket fall open. He remembered the weight and feel of her smooth, silky breasts and how the softest touch would arouse her. He focused on her face, not daring to look at his tented pants. He'd been semi-erect since the moment he'd started talking to her at the courthouse, and being held hostage didn't seem to have any effect on his lust.

No wonder she taunted him. She hadn't betrayed him by becoming a defense attorney. He had refused to listen and then dumped her, which made her physical reaction to him even more surprising. "What was last night about?"

"Apparently, you're still my kryptonite. It's a flaw. I'm working on it.

She sounded so disheartened he almost smiled. "Don't you hate it when that happens?"

"It would be helpful in the future if we avoided each other."

"You're kidding?" He wasn't going anywhere and hated she didn't want to see him again.

She shrugged one shoulder. It was an oddly provocative action. "It was worth a shot. Look, there's no future for us. We're all chemistry and no substance, and I need substance." Her smile wavered, making him wonder if she was as conflicted in her feelings for him as he was for her.

"What do you mean by substance?"

"You know, couples who build something lasting are about more than just sex. They support each other when things get tough. They talk about—"

"Feelings." He almost rolled his eyes but contained the impulse.

"Maybe. Look, we're good at the physical thing, but any man can give me that. I want more. I want something real. Let's face it, a man who can't even acknowledge me in public is never going to give me the kind of relationship I need."

His parents had the kind of rapport she was talking about, but he'd never experienced it. The only time he'd even come close was with Sophia. He remembered her face when they'd split. He could still see the pain in her eyes, the anguish. They'd argued over her choice of career, and he'd given her an ultimatum. *Help put the bad guys away or we're through.*

Who'd have thought all these years later he'd be begging for her help to save an innocent kid? The fact that she'd agreed to take the case, in spite of their past, showed her commitment to the justice system. A system he hadn't fully appreciated until now.

He opened his mouth to tell her she was right but stopped when Old Woman marched into the lobby, his demeanor efficient and military. He had drywall dust on his clothing, hands, and arms. His right hand held an AR-15 assault rifle. Unlike the other robbers, he wasn't wearing gloves, which meant he either wasn't in the system or wasn't worried about getting caught. Cases where criminals burned off their fingerprints were rare because the procedure tended to cause nerve damage. There was another option, but Mateo had only read about it. Adermatoglyphia, a condition where people were born without fingerprints.

Old Woman aimed his weapon directly at Mateo's head. "Let's go, lover boy. It's time to talk to the cops. We're ready to negotiate."

CHAPTER FIVE

Sophia gasped as Old woman forced Mateo to his feet and marched him across the bank to a phone that sat on the receptionist's desk. *They're not going to kill him. They're not going to kill him.* She repeated the words, hoping they were true.

Old woman pressed his weapon against the base of Mateo's skull. "You're going to tell them exactly what I say. You will not add anything. You will not change a word. If you try to be clever, I will shoot you."

Sophia flinched. She remembered the feel of the steel barrel against her temple and knew firsthand how terrifying it was to know that with, one twitch of the finger, she would be dead.

Mateo cut a hate-filled gaze to his captor. "Release the hostages. You have me. I'm a cop. You don't need them."

Using the butt of the gun, Old Woman struck Mateo on the back of the head. He stumbled awkwardly and fell to the floor, his bound hands no help in stopping him. He groaned as he landed on his right shoulder and then stilled, his chest heaving.

"Baby, bring the lawyer." Old Woman grabbed Mateo by his shirt collar, twisting it so the garment choked him. "Do you really think you're in any position to bargain?" Old Woman shouted.

He released Mateo and then switched his rifle to his other hand. Before Mateo could catch his breath, Old Woman punched him in the stomach. He coughed as he curled into a protective ball.

The man with the baby mask grabbed her arm and yanked her to her feet. She tripped, trying to find her footing as he dragged her across the room until she stood beside Mateo, who was now on his feet and bent at the waist. His breath came in loud gasps.

Baby released his hold on her and returned to his post near the front door.

Old Woman rammed the rifle against the nape of her neck with a force that made her wince. She yelped as pain simultaneously radiated down her spine and up into her skull. Her legs turned to jelly. The ceiling seemed to be crashing down on her. She wished she could run away and escape this nightmare. She inhaled deeply, counted to eight, and then exhaled, praying for some much needed restraint.

"You're a pretty thing, but you won't look as good without your head." Using the barrel of the gun, Old Woman pushed her forward.

"Let's try this again." Old Woman sneered at Mateo. "If you don't tell the fucking police exactly what I say, I'll kill the woman. Then I will kill another hostage and another. But I'll start with the one that matters most. Do you understand?"

Sophia swallowed, but the lump remained in her throat. She wished she could stop shaking, but her body wouldn't obey her commands. She tensed her muscles in a desperate attempt at control. *Get a grip*.

Mateo's gaze snagged hers. A range of emotions shone in his eyes—anger, fear, maybe even regret. He turned to Old Woman. "Okay."

The phone rang again.

Old Woman reached out, but stopped, his hand an inch away. "Remember you will repeat my words exactly."

"Yes." Mateo's voice was flat, emotionless.

Old Woman pressed a button, putting the phone on speaker.

"Hello this is Captain Tate. Who am I talking to?"

Mateo looked at Old Woman for guidance.

Old Woman gave a slight nod.

"I'm Detective Mateo Ramirez."

Old Woman then pressed the gun harder against her neck. She muffled a cry.

"Are you a hostage?"

Old Woman nodded again.

"Yes." Mateo was tense, rigid.

"I want to speak to whoever's in charge."

Old woman shook his head.

"They said no."

"Are they forcing you to talk?"

Old Woman nodded.

"Yes."

"What do they want?" Captain Tate was all business. He was new to the police department. Sophia hadn't worked on any of his cases. She had no idea what kind of a man he was or if he was trained for this situation.

Mateo looked at Old Woman and shrugged, silently asking for an answer.

Old Woman fished a prewritten index card from the pocket of his sweatshirt and held it up for Mateo to read.

Mateo's eyes widened. "They want ten million dollars by midnight."

Old Woman threw the card on the floor and then pulled out another card.

Mateo shook his head slightly as if denying the request and then said, "And they want a helicopter." He probably had his doubts about their ability to comply with the request.

Old Woman eased the gun away so it was no longer jammed against her neck. She turned slightly so she could use her peripheral vision to observe him. She had interviewed a lot of witnesses both on and off the stand and had come to know when their words didn't match their emotions. It was a gift, one that had helped her earn the reputation as the best defense attorney in the city. Old Woman was lying about the money and about the helicopter. She couldn't exactly say why she knew that. Maybe it was the way he held his body or the egotistical glint in his eyes.

"Ten million and a helicopter," Tate said, repeating the request. "My bosses are never going to go for that unless you give me something in return. A show of good faith."

Old Woman shook his head.

Mateo answered. "He said no."

"How many hostages do you have?"

Old Woman held up yet another card.

"Twenty," Mateo repeated. Once again, he shook his head in an almost imperceptible movement.

The number wasn't right. There were ten patrons and five staff, which meant there were seventeen captives including herself and Mateo.

"Maybe you can release the women and the elderly?" Captain Tate's irritatingly calm voice echoed over the line.

Old Woman seemed to be prepared for every question and didn't even need to sort through his replies to get the right answer. It was as though he'd read the hostage negotiation handbook and had arranged his responses accordingly.

"He'll think about it," Mateo said.

Old Woman pressed a button and disconnected the call.

She breathed a sigh of relief as Old Woman stepped back, no longer pointing his weapon at her. "Go and sit."

She did as she was told, returning to her spot on the floor near the teller's window.

Old Woman stood in front of Mateo, his stance confrontational. "You put your woman in danger. Is that any way to treat a lady?"

Before Mateo could answer, he bashed the butt of the gun into Mateo's face. Mateo stumbled, but remained on his feet.

"Go and sit with her," Old woman ordered. "Next time I expect compliance."

There was something about Old Woman's word choices that made Sophia take notice. He'd used the word *compliance* instead of *do as I say.* That wasn't much, but an impression was starting to form of someone who was well educated, or at least well read, and highly intelligent. This robbery was well planned, and these weren't your everyday thieves.

Mateo groaned as he slumped down next to her. The right side of his face and eye were already starting to swell and turn a deep shade of purple.

"Are you okay?" She itched to put her arms around him and offer comfort, but the best she could do was rest her forehead against his, being careful not to bump his welts.

Mateo tried to smile and then winced with the effort. "I'll be fine. I've been hurt worse."

"You were right when you said earlier that these guys have a plan. I think they're playing for time," she whispered.

As he pulled away, his gaze met hers. She'd expected to see anger and determination, but all she saw was regret. "I'm sorry I was rude to you at work. I should've been nicer."

She didn't know how to react. She'd been angry that he ignored her and greeted her as if he didn't want to be seen with her, but this felt like surrender. As though he wanted to make things right before they killed him.

"You stop that right now," she hissed, keeping her voice low so their captors wouldn't hear. "We're getting out of this."

"Yes ma'am."

She was relieved to see a spark of hope in his eyes.

He sucked in a deep breath and straightened, as though just the act of breathing had given him strength. Then he smiled. "You're something else, Sophia Reed. No wonder you're so good in the sack."

CHAPTER SIX

FBI Supervisory Special Agent Finn Callaghan stood near Captain Tate, not offering any suggestions. The area around the bank had been cordoned off. Red and blue lights from the surrounding police cruisers lit the night sky. A fire truck and ambulance were on scene just in case. He could feel the pressure in the air. Word that Detective Ramirez was being held captive was now common knowledge, increasing the tension.

As one of only two agents assigned to the Granite City Resident Agency, it wasn't unusual for him to work closely with local law enforcement. But in this case, he didn't have any advice to give. He wasn't a trained negotiator. He was an investigator who was good at conducting interviews and reading body language. Other officers in the Granite City-Elkhead County Police Department whispered about him being a human lie detector, but that wasn't true. It was almost impossible to tell when someone was lying, mainly because people fibbed every day. From an early age, they were conditioned to tell lies, not because the general population was inherently deceitful, but because telling someone what they wanted to hear made them feel better, and more often than not, kept the peace.

Captain Tate approached, holding out a packet of sugar-free gum, offering Finn a piece. Finn declined.

Tate's graying blond hair lifted in the breeze. He was trim for a man in his forties, his athletic build a testament to his workout addiction. If it weren't for his bulbous nose and pockmarked face, he would've been an attractive man. He stuffed a piece of gum in his mouth and started chewing. "They want ten million and a helicopter by midnight."

Finn let out a low whistle. That was a tall order. "There's no way we can get that kind of money in three hours. Are they willing to release any of the hostages?" The most important goal in these situations was getting the people out alive.

"They said they'll think about releasing the women and elderly but my gut says no. Do you have any insights?" He worked the gum, chomping harder. He was covering as the interim police chief. The last chief stood accused of public corruption after he had covered up attempts by a local businessman to kill Finn's friends, David Quinn and Marie Wilson. Finn had played a role in the investigation, so had Detective Ramirez.

Finn shook his head. "No. How many captives have your spotters counted?"

"The building is a hundred years old. Back then, windows were expensive." He pointed to the bank with its ornate stone columns.

Somehow it reminded Finn of the Alder Planetarium in Chicago. It didn't have the dome roof and it wasn't circular, but the granite façade coupled with the lack of windows did speak to a bygone era. There was a thin glass pane above the front door. He imagined the interior to be dark and oppressive with very little natural light. "So your snipers can't see in?"

"No, and we need to know what's going on." If Tate was frustrated with the situation, it didn't show. He was a professional who was focused on doing his job.

"I'm willing to call in FBI resources. What do you need?" Finn knew his superiors in Salt Lake City would be more than happy to help, considering this was a hostage situation with innocent lives at stake.

"We need technical help. I want to see and hear the bad guys. I need to know every move they make."

"I can understand that." If he were in the same situation, he would need accurate information so he could make informed decisions.

Tate massaged the back of his neck, working out the kinks. "I'm trained to respond to this in four different ways." He held up one finger. "I could opt for a confrontational response."

"You've done that," Finn stated, looking at the Granite City-Elkhead County police officers amassed in front of the bank, each of them carrying considerable firepower, ready for an assault.

Tate held up a second finger, seemingly needing to discuss the scene and the choices at his disposal. "I usually prefer to use selective sniper fire."

Finn didn't mind. Sometimes it helped to talk through the variables. "I agree. A sniper is usually the best choice. That way we can take out the bad guys with no unnecessary casualties." He glanced at the bank. It was more like a bunker than a place of business. "But that's not an option in this case, is it?"

Captain Tate gave a curt nod. "I don't want to use chemical agents either. We have no idea how many hostages they have, and we also don't know the condition of their health. They said twenty, but who knows if they're telling the truth."

"That only leaves negotiation." In Finn's opinion, this was the most frustrating choice.

The captain spat out his gum. "I hate negotiating."

"I thought you were a trained negotiator." Finn ignored the chewed-up glob lying on the sidewalk.

"I am, but there are a lot of things that can go wrong. You never know what kind of psycho you're dealing with. One misspoken word or nonverbal cue can derail the whole thing and make him kill everyone inside."

Finn grabbed his phone from the pocket of his cargo pants. "Let me make a call and see what I can get to help."

Special Agent Kennedy Morris picked up on the first ring. "Hi, boss."

Finn didn't bother with small talk. "I need you to call Salt Lake City. See what you can get in terms of infrared and listening equipment. This place is built like a bomb shelter. We can't see or hear anything."

"How many hostages?" Kennedy was incisive and intelligent. She might have been born with the proverbial silver spoon in her mouth, but as an ex-marine, she was more than capable of getting her hands dirty if required.

"They say twenty, including Ramirez."

Her voice rose when she said, "Detective Ramirez?"

"Yes." The perpetrators knew Ramirez was a cop. That meant one of two things. They were either beating the crap out of him in an attempt at revenge or they would leave him alone. It all depended on whether they planned to live and serve a sentence, or if they felt they had nothing to lose.

"I'll make the calls now," Kennedy said, understanding the implications without explanation. "We're a long way from headquarters. It might take a while to get the equipment up here."

"See what you can do. They've given us until midnight." It was nearly nine o'clock now, which meant they had three hours.

Finn disconnected and addressed Tate. "You need to play for time."

A young officer, who didn't look old enough to shave, addressed them, "Sirs." He almost bowed. "You should listen to this."

Tate clenched his jaw, biting off a curse. "I don't have time—"

"No, sir, this is important." The patrolman wasn't taking no for an answer.

Finn had to hand it to him. He had stones. There

weren't many cops who would talk to their superior with that tone.

"One of the captives is on the radio." The kid reached into a nearby squad car and turned a dial, increasing the volume.

"And you say you're a hostage?" The smooth voice of the announcer came through loud and clear.

"Y-y-yes." A woman's weepy voice filled the air.

"What's your name?"

"Elena."

"Hi Elena, tell us about yourself."

"I'm a mom. I-I…" She sobbed, her cries heart-breaking in their intensity. Then she sniffled, re-gaining her composure. "I want to tell my son, Jacob, I love him."

"How old is Jacob?" The radio host had softened his tone.

"Two." Another sob.

"I'll make sure he gets the message. You're in my thoughts and prayers as are the other hostages."

"I have to give the police a message." Her voice cracked on the last word.

"Will the men who are holding you talk to me?"

There was silence for a moment followed by a muffled sound in the background. "N-no."

"Okay, what's the message," the host continued.

"The police have until midnight to get the money and the helicopter. After that, they're going to start shooting," she wailed.

The line went dead.

Finn turned to Tate. "Shit."

Tate thumped the roof of the car. "Those bastards are planning to kill everyone. I'd bet my next pay check."

"Why do you think that?" Finn was horrified by the possibility that the captain could be right.

"In a hostage negotiation, you take small steps. You try to establish trust. You give them something they want in return for a concession. The best exchanges result in the release of captives. These guys have demanded money and a helicopter, but that's all it is—demands. They're not communicating. I could send in food, offer to go in there myself—there's a whole book's worth of different options. But these guys are laying on the pressure without actually negotiating."

"They might give you instructions closer to the time." Finn didn't like how this was playing out.

Tate cracked his knuckles as he stared at the besieged bank. "Maybe, but they've made my job ten times harder because now I have to deal with a media shitshow. I'm surprised the mayor hasn't called."

The captain's cell phone vibrated in his pocket. He took it out and looked at the screen. "There's the mayor, right on cue. Perhaps that's their plan, to put me under so much pressure I'll fold and let them fly out of here in a helicopter with the hostages and money."

CHAPTER SEVEN

Mateo found the booming and crashing noises that came from the vault area of the bank somewhat comforting. It meant the robbers hadn't finished. Two of them were working in the back while the third, Baby, acted as sentry. He paced in a circle around the small entrance, ignoring the hostages. Occasionally, he would glance at his phone, making Mateo wonder if they had access to street-cams or had placed some kind of surveillance camera outside.

The phone on the reception desk kept ringing, but the gang ignored it. Mateo knew his superiors in law enforcement would try to negotiate their release, but that didn't seem to be Old Woman's goal. Mateo couldn't see a clock from his position in front of the teller's window, but estimated it had been at least two hours since he'd talked to Captain Tate, which would make it about ten o'clock.

He stared at the ground in an attempt to block out all distractions and concentrate. He had to work out what was going on before the robbery was complete. Old Woman had given Tate until midnight, which meant he had two hours to come up with a plan. That was only true if Old Woman kept his word about the deadline, but Mateo had his doubts about the sincerity of Old Woman's promises. Once the dirt bags were done, they would no longer need their prisoners. That would leave them with two choices. They could release the captives or kill them. He had no idea how they would respond.

The receptionist had been forced to make the call to the radio station, which was interesting. It put a very sympathetic face on the situation and would place a burden on the police to resolve the problem quickly. He could see why they'd used the young woman, Elena. Even now when everything was relatively calm, he could hear her sobbing over the sound of the robbers plundering the bank. Her long dark hair hung over her face, and her eyes were puffy and inflamed.

Old Woman wanted someone who would tug at the public's heartstrings, and who better than a frightened mother? Everyone would want Elena to live, as they should. But there was something calculated about it. Mateo felt like he was watching a drama unfold rather than seeing an instinctive response. He got the impression they had prepared for every possibility, which meant they had probably observed the staff, done thorough background checks, and rehearsed in order to execute the perfect crime.

"What do you think they have planned?" Sophia asked, as if reading his mind.

"I don't know, but the hardest part of any robbery is getting away with the money. Think of the weight and volume. They have to carry whatever is in the safety deposit boxes, plus the cash from the safe. I assume there's enough of a haul for it to be heavy and cumbersome. He nodded at the bank manager, trying to attract his attention. But the pale, portly man turned his head and looked the other way.

"Damn." All he wanted was information. He wasn't going to ask an out-of-shape civilian to take on an armed gunman.

"He's not going to help you," Sophia said, "And you'd understand why if you could see your face."

He flexed his jaw, feeling the swelling around his right eye, cheek, and lip. That bad, huh?"

She scrunched her face and then said, "You've looked better."

He almost laughed. "That's the most diplomatic thing you've ever said to me."

"Are you saying I'm blunt?"

"Yes, but not mean. You just say what's on your mind."

She sighed. "I save all my diplomacy for judges. I don't have any left for the people in my life."

"Do you have many people in your life?" He should probably concentrate on their captors, but somehow finding out about her world seemed just as important. He hadn't thought to ask her if she had anyone special. She was too straightforward to be duplicitous. He was pretty sure if she had a partner, last night would never have happened.

She was right; they were all chemistry and no substance. They didn't know each other because he had wasted years being a blind fool.

"A few. Jane, my receptionist, is my closest friend. You must've seen her yesterday." She blushed, probably remembering their encounter.

"Yes, she told me to go right in and then grabbed her purse. Did you tell her about us?"

"Of course, I told her what a rat-bastard jerk you are. What about you? Do you have any family?" She'd changed the subject. He would've liked to question his role as the rat-bastard jerk, but he deserved the title so there was no point.

"My parents are retired and live in Butte. My brother's married. He's a carpenter who works building film sets in LA. I haven't seen him in ages." He missed his brother. It had been way too long since they'd spoken. Mateo knew the lack of contact with his family was his fault. He gave everything he had to the job and didn't make time for family and friends. That was why Andrea-the-bitch had cheated on him and then divorced him. Although, in his defense, working had been better than going home and listening to her complain about the size of his salary. "If I get out of here, I'm going to take a trip to California and see him."

"You mean *when* not *if*."

It had been a poor choice of words and not a reflection of his mindset, but he liked how she wouldn't let him get away with anything.

She turned her gaze toward the vault area.

The constant hammering continued to reverberate through the bank. "Whatever they're doing back there is labor-intensive." She studied him for a moment. "You said earlier the hardest part of a bank robbery is getting away. Do you think they have a plan to escape?"

"Definitely. I would love to know how. It would be standard operating procedure for the police to have the bank surrounded. They would also have the SWAT team on standby. Maybe our masked men are counting on that helicopter, but I don't think so. That means they're either going to use the hostages as a human shield or they've tunneled under the bank. My money would be on the hostages."

"Why not the tunnel?"

"Because you would need specialized equipment, and building a tunnel is a lot more complicated than you'd think. They would have to blast through rock, and the ground might not be stable. It's just not a viable option."

Her brow crinkled. "Not necessarily."

"What do you mean?"

"About a hundred years ago, the town burned down. The residents decided it was too risky to rebuild wood houses in a place where there were no firefighters, so they built their residences and businesses underground."

"Are you trying to tell me there's a business network under Granite City that no one knows about? That's ridiculous."

"There was one, but it's not there anymore. The

tunnels fell into disrepair. Eventually, they were closed up and the entrances were sealed. I only know about them because I did a local history course when I was at university. The town of Harve has similar tunnels, and there are three miles of underground streams running under Billings. And some say Missoula—"

"I get it. These guys could've accessed the tunnels and then what? Made a hole from the tunnel into the bank? That's still a lot of work." He hoped she was right, even though the idea seemed far-fetched. He would love for them to disappear without harming anyone.

Sophia rocked back and forth as she stared at the ground, thinking. It was a small movement, probably a self-soothing mechanism. "Do you think they'll get their ten million ransom?"

"Not a chance." He didn't hesitate. There wasn't enough time for the police to get hold of that much money. The unreasonable demand made him uneasy. It was as though an alarm was blaring at the back of his mind, warning him. But he didn't know how he should react or what he could do to protect the hostages.

"And why did they say there were twenty of us?" Sophia turned to stare at the people sitting on the floor. After hours of terror, sitting bound on the hardwood floor, with no bathroom breaks, every one of them looked worn-out, pale, and traumatized.

"I have no idea. With enough time, the department will get their hands on some infrared equipment. They're going to know exactly how many people are in here and what they're doing." The security cameras were high up on the ceiling. He couldn't tell if they were turned on or not. "I noticed our criminals haven't covered the surveillance equipment."

She stopped rocking and looked up. "What does that mean?"

"Nothing really. They probably used a Wi-Fi connection. You block the link, and you're all set. Everything's blank."

She shook her head. "I bet they have an old-fashioned feed to a recording device and they're still on, but the police can't access them."

"Why do you say that?"

"Because they wouldn't be wearing masks if they weren't worried about being seen." She rolled her neck from side to side, trying to relieve some of the tension. He understood how she felt.

Stabbing pain shot through the muscles of his shoulders, neck, back, and arms. And no matter how much he wiggled his fingers, they still tingled from lack of circulation. "Good point. I hope it means they plan to release us, and they don't want anyone to be able to identify them."

She rocked back and forth again. "Do you think they'll use the tunnels?"

"I don't know. I didn't even know they existed until you mentioned them. For the record, I hope you're right. I hope they escape through the tunnels and leave the rest of us behind." A tension headache began to form behind his eyes. He inhaled deeply and then exhaled, forcing himself to relax.

She shifted closer to him and leaned in. "I still have my smartwatch. We could use that to send a message."

"How did you manage to hide that?" He couldn't contain his surprise. Baby still circled the lobby and didn't react to his outburst. He turned his attention back to Sophia, lowering his voice. "That was a terrible risk."

She shrugged. She wasn't rocking anymore. For the first time, he wondered if the self-soothing was a reaction to their inactivity rather than fear. She had obviously been willing to take a chance and hide the device, but what if they'd caught her?

There was no point in thinking like that. She had the watch. He could contact the department. It would be helpful for law enforcement to know the number of hostages, the weaponry, and how many bad guys they were up against.

"Scoot around so I can see it." Accessing the watch while bound would be a challenge.

They wiggled on the ground until she sat with her back to him and he could reach her wrist with his hands. It was slow going. He wasn't familiar with the settings. He had to stop and twist around so he could see what he was doing. He had almost finished entering Captain Tate's cell number when the banging stopped.

The silence was ominous. A warning. The next

phase of their captor's plan was about to be enacted.

CHAPTER EIGHT

Mateo grabbed Sophia's sleeve and tugged it down her arm. They worked to right themselves, sliding on their butts so they sat with their backs to the wall.

Old Woman marched into the lobby. He pointed his AR-15 semi-automatic rifle at the ceiling and shot off a few rounds.

Mateo threw his body over Sophia, who pushed against him, shoving him to the side.

The hostages in the middle of the room seemed to jerk in unison. Elena screamed and wailed.

"Everyone stand," Old Woman shouted.

Those who could struggled to their knees. From that position, they were able to stand. Baby grabbed an elderly gentleman by the arm and jerked him up. The man had white hair, a bent frame, and the sagging skin of an eighty-year old. He winced in pain.

The octogenarian had to be in agony after being bound for so long, but Mateo was pleased to see defiance in his eyes.

Old Man pulled a combat knife from a scabbard attached to his belt and sliced through the hostage's ties one by one. The pieces of plastic fell to the ground. All of the captives rubbed their wrists and shoulders, an action Mateo knew was not only a reflex, but helped ease the pain endured by the restraints.

Mateo along with Sophia rose to their feet. Their movements were clumsy and awkward.

Together they stepped toward the people in the middle of the lobby, waiting their turn for their bonds to be cut.

"You two stay where you are," Old Woman said as he swung the rifle toward them. "I have other plans for you."

Old Man stood behind Sophia and efficiently cut through her bindings. Then he marched to the front of the lobby and grabbed his tote bag.

"What about Mateo?" Sophia protested. "Aren't you going to untie him?"

Old Woman struck her across the face with the back of his hand. She fell against Mateo. He used his body to prevent her from crashing into the wall.

"Leave her alone!" Without thinking, he bent at the waist and charged Old Woman like a ram in rutting season. He didn't need his hands to beat a coward. He could do the job with his head and his feet.

A blow came from behind, throwing him off balance. The second strike knocked him to the ground. He thought he heard screaming but couldn't be sure because his ears were ringing. The third hit to his head made him see stars. Then Old Woman kicked him in the ribs, forcing air from his lungs. He gasped for breath.

Sophia threw herself over him, shielding him

with her body. "Don't you dare touch him!" She cradled him in her arms.

He tried to speak. He wanted her to leave and save herself, but his words were slurred and incoherent.

Old Woman grabbed Sophia, wrenching her away.

Mateo could see her struggling in his peripheral vision. He pushed himself up on his elbow. The action made his stomach heave and his vision blur.

Old Woman bent over. He was so close Mateo could smell his rancid breath. "Don't worry, Ramirez. You're getting what you want. The hostages are going free, and the price for their freedom is your girlfriend. I'm taking her with me."

"No." Mateo tried to shout, but his voice was no more than a croak.

Sophia fought as Old Woman dragged her away. "Mateo," she screamed. "It would never have worked between us. Aunt Valerie will always be number one!"

Mateo groaned. He needed to stop them. Sooner or later, their masks would come off, and if she was present when that happened, they would have to kill her. There was also the possibility the one with the old man mask would rape her. His stomach rolled again at the idea. He needed her to be safe and happy, even if they weren't together. He staggered to his knees.

"Some people don't know when to give up. This is for your own good." Old Man kicked him in the kidneys.

Pain ricocheted through Mateo's body as he was thrown forward and landed face down on the hard wooden floor. He gave an involuntary grunt and then froze, using all his willpower to stay still. He closed his eyes, pretending to be unconscious. If he gave them a reason, they would beat him again, and he would be no good to anyone if he was dead. He had to conserve his energy to save Sophia.

He held his position, listening for his captor's footsteps. When he estimated they were on the other side of the lobby, he opened his eyes a fraction. Even the small sliver of light hurt. The world spun, and he was thankful he was lying down. He probably had a concussion. He tried to remember the symptoms—nausea, headache, fatigue... What else? He needed to know. He had to prepare himself mentally so he could work through it and find Sophia.

He tried opening his eyes again, steeling himself against the pain.

Baby crossed the lobby and set a duct-taped bundle of spray-paint cans at the cashier's window. He tied a long cloth to the package, pulled some matches from his pocket, and lit the rag.

Mateo pretended to be comatose as Baby grabbed him by both arms and dragged him across the floor so he lay under the burning device.

Damn. He would bet good money they were planning to create a fireball. Mateo had seen videos on social media. The blogger had shot a spray paint canister, which exploded into a burning corkscrew. The people who'd posted the footage had been outside in a location where there was enough area for the spiraling inferno to bounce around without causing serious injury. To set off something like that in the enclosed space of the bank was beyond dangerous.

If they were planning to burn him alive, he would need to move. Once the bullet struck the cylinders, the reaction would be almost instantaneous. Mateo sat up. Pretending to be unconscious was no longer in his best interests. The movement made everything blur. He blinked and was thankful when the world came into focus.

Baby pulled out a handgun and stepped back ten feet, aiming his weapon. He was either going to shoot Mateo or the spray paint. It didn't matter which target Baby hit. There was a good chance Mateo would be injured either way.

He rolled, trying to put as much distance between him and the shooter as possible. A clunk sounded as Baby's shot hit the cans, and then there was a loud hiss as a ball of flame curled into the air. Burning paint jettisoned through the bullet hole, hurling the inferno upward. It crashed into the ceiling with a boom and landed behind and to the left of the teller's workspace.

Old Man reached into his tote and grabbed three short green tubes with the words *Smoke Grenade* printed on them in large letters. He pulled the rings and threw the grenades at the screaming captives, who were now running to the front of the bank. Then he and Baby retreated down the hallway to the right, heading to the vault area.

Mateo could hear yelling as the hostages hammered on the door. His eyes itched and stung as a gray haze enveloped him. He staggered to his feet, stumbled, and then fell to his knees. He coughed as smoke burned his throat.

Old Woman had taken Sophia. That thought sliced through him. He stilled, trying to come up with a plan. He had to find her. Even though she'd made it clear they could never be together, he needed to know she was safe. He couldn't comprehend a world without her.

He coughed again when the thick fumes clogged his airways. Shouts and banging echoed through the bank as the hostages tried desperately to escape. He headed away from the noise. He aimed for the hallway that led to the vault, but was blocked by a wall of flame. A flash of fire threw him back as the blaze spread to the ceiling, burning everything in its path.

Heat singed his face. There was no way he could get to Sophia. He needed a better strategy. He shuffled low to the ground toward the front door with his hands still tied behind his back. He stumbled, but managed to balance on his knees, and followed the sound of screams, praying he was headed in the right direction. He had to make it out. He had to live so he could save Sophia.

CHAPTER NINE

Finn Callaghan clung to the sliver of hope that the hostage takers would negotiate, but that hope was fading. Captain Tate had been calling them for hours, but they hadn't picked up the phone, and there was only an hour left until midnight.

Tate clutched a large bag that contained three million dollars. The mayor had arranged for the money to be delivered to the police. Finn didn't know how the mayor came by the money, and this wasn't the time to ask.

"How the hell am I supposed to exchange the people for cash if they won't answer the phone?" Tate chewed heavily on his last piece of gum.

"Are your men ready?" Finn asked. It was a stupid question. He could see that the SWAT team had been ready since the standoff began, but he believed in crossing his *Ts*.

Tate chewed some more as he threw the bag of money into the front seat of his cruiser. "This will end badly. We'll be going in blind, and that's never good. Have you heard anything from Salt Lake City?"

"Only that the Hostage Rescue Team is on the way." The Hostage Rescue Team, or HRT as it was known, was an elite unit within the FBI who conducted rescues worldwide. They had the equipment, training, and tactical helicopter needed to handle this situation.

Finn breathed a sigh of relief when he heard the whirl of helicopter blades overhead.

"This is HRT 1 to Granite City Police." The disembodied voice crackled over the radio in Tate's vehicle.

Tate dived into the car. "This is Captain Tate. Go ahead."

"We're over the target."

Finn watched as the powerful helicopter searchlights flashed on.

"Sir, the bank is hot."

Tate clicked the mic. "What do you mean 'hot'?"

"I mean it's on fire. There's a massive heat signature at the rear of the structure."

"What about the hostages?" Tate spat out his gum.

"They're trapped near the front door."

"Any sign of dirt bags with weapons?"

"Negative."

Tate dropped the radio and ran to the roadblock. "Let the fire truck through."

Officer's scrambled to their cruisers, rushing to obey Tate's command. The fire truck, siren's blaring, raced through the barricade.

A loud whoosh sounded, followed by the crack of shattering glass as a skylight exploded. The screams of the trapped hostages rang out.

"Get them out," Tate shouted at the firemen who were running for the building, axes in hand.

Finn grabbed Tate's arm. "We need to contain them in case the kidnappers try to use the confusion to escape."

Tate shouted orders to his men, setting up a perimeter.

The HRT team still hovered above. They had infrared and night vision technology. There was no way the bad guys could get away.

CHAPTER TEN

"Please let me go and help them," Sophia pleaded as Old Woman shoved her ahead of him into the vault that housed the safety deposit boxes. It was wrecked. All the little doors were open. Some of them were bent; others were hanging by a hinge. Trays had been emptied and scattered about the floor.

The sound of people crying for help became louder, more intense, as wafts of smoke drifted into the room.

"Don't worry," Old Woman said. "If the firemen can chop through the door in time, they'll all be saved."

He hadn't removed his disguise. Sophia wasn't sure if that was significant. She coughed as the smoke burned her throat. How was Mateo coping? He was injured. She'd heard the sickening sounds of Baby and Old Man beating him as Old Woman dragged her away. He could be lying unconscious with no way to save himself.

She eyed the door. Shadows moved and flickered as the flames grew and danced just out of sight. If she made a run for it, she might be able to get to him.

"Don't even think about bolting. I will shoot

you." Old Woman nudged her toward the back of the room.

The screams grew louder, followed by the sound of splintering wood. She needed the element of surprise if she was going to escape, but that was gone because she'd been too stupid to use her poker face. Her breathing hitched. "Please, let me go. He'll die." She didn't care that she was begging, didn't care about anything except Mateo.

Old Woman didn't answer. Instead, he placed a hand between her shoulders and propelled her toward a man-sized hole that was located in the ground at the rear of the room. It was deep with layers revealing flooring, concrete, and dirt.

She backed up, resisting, knowing if she went into that pit, she might never come back. Surprisingly, Old Woman didn't strike her or yell at her. He simply stepped around and tossed a large tote over the edge. Maybe they would leave her here. Then she could go back for Mateo.

She glanced around, searching for any specialized equipment they might have used, and saw a large drill in the corner. "You cut through this in a couple of hours?"

"We did most of it before. We only had the last little bit to do today," Old woman said as he pitched another bag over the edge.

She had been wondering aloud and hadn't expected an answer. It was alarming how reasonable, methodical, and calm Old Woman sounded, especially when measured against the yelling of the captives and the chaos caused by the fire.

She coughed as ash particles drifted through the air, propelled by the increasing heat. Did the authorities even know about the tunnels? Someone might, but they weren't common knowledge. It could take days before they sorted out the mess. By that time, Old Woman and the others would be long gone.

Baby and Old Man climbed down a rope ladder into the void below.

Old Woman heaved the last two tote bags into the tunnel. Then he pointed to the ladder. "Your turn."

She glanced back toward the bank. Flames licked the door and inched along the ceiling. Mateo might even be unconscious. She needed him and hoped one day he would need her. Even if there was never anything more than sex between them, she wanted him to be alive, not dead at the hands of these criminals. She shook her head. "I'm not leaving without Mateo."

Old Woman grabbed her arm in a vice-like grip. "You can climb down the ladder or I will throw you down. You choose."

Mateo's life mattered more than whatever torture this animal could inflict on her.

She kicked Old Woman in the shins. He yelped and released her. She ran for the door. She only managed to make it a few feet when Old Woman caught up with her. He grabbed her by her jacket and threw her down the hole.

****

A wall of flames and smoke prevented Mateo from running back into the building to find Sophia. Two firefighters had dragged him away and forced him into the ambulance. He wanted to help fight the fire, find her and hold her close. The thought that she might burn to death hollowed out his insides, leaving him desolate.

Emergency personnel covered the area like ants at a picnic. Firemen had broken open the door, freeing the hostages from the ravaged building. The police were searching and interviewing them, checking identities and taking witness statements.

The dirt bags had known what they were doing when they gave the wrong headcount. Law enforcement had no idea if one of the victims was really one of the bad guys.

He was surprised they hadn't questioned him first. He was trained to be observant and had spent time with his attackers. He had information they needed, but for some unknown reason, he'd been dismissed, sidelined in an ambulance with a blanket wrapped around him, breathing into an oxygen mask. He would talk to the captain and make him listen. The police needed to know about the tunnels. He stood. His vision blurred, and his legs threatened to give out. He sat back down, gasping for breath, and blinked back tears, wiping his eyes with the back of his hand. The smoke must be making them water. *Damn.* Now he was lying to himself.

There was no way anyone could survive the

heat and smoke. He hoped they had escaped underground and Old Woman and his crew weren't trying to last out the blaze in the vault. If that were the case, then Sophia was dead. His chest tightened. The inferno was so severe there were three fire trucks on the scene now.

It didn't matter that she might be right about the tunnels because they couldn't access them. It would take hours if not days before they could extinguish the fire. By that time, the bastards would be long gone. And what would happen to Sophia? What did they plan to do with her?

Her last words echoed through his mind. *It would never have worked between us. Aunt Valerie will always be number one.* He understood her Aunt Valerie must be important to her. She was, after all, the woman who had taken them in when her father was wrongfully imprisoned. But why would she sacrifice her future happiness for her aunt? Why had she rejected him? He liked to think he could've changed her mind and persuaded her to give him another chance.

He imagined running his hands through her fine pale brown hair. He loved the way it hung about her face. She was a woman of contradictions. In the courtroom, she was all business. As a lawyer she was powerful and formidable and somewhat reserved. Prosecutors groaned when they learned she was working for the defense. Some of them had even named her the Pitbull. Once she got her teeth into a case, she didn't let go. But when they were alone she was sexy, exciting, and sweet.

He wanted to be the only man in her life, the only one to see her sensuous side. It might be a caveman response, but denying it wouldn't make it go away.

There was so much more to her than sex. She knew who she was and lived her life by her own rules. She was a defense attorney because she believed everyone was innocent until proven guilty and wanted the law to reflect that principle.

No matter how much it might frustrate him when someone he considered a criminal walked, it was the American system of justice. That was why he had gone to her office yesterday. He needed an attorney to defend a kid he knew was innocent. He swallowed as a lump formed in his throat. He had wasted so much time ignoring her, hating the fact she worked for the opposite side when, in reality, they both worked for the same team.

The bank was now a burning shell. The stone walls still stood, but the interior and roof were engulfed. Flames shot into the night sky and through the tiny crevices left by the shattered windows. Occasionally, the sound of the interior collapsing or an explosion could be heard above the constant crackle and hiss of flames.

Even if it was pure make-believe, he imagined she was alive somewhere. *Aunt Valerie will always be number one.* He stood, allowing the blanket to fall to the ground.

Damn, Sophia was smart, way smarter than him.

He flipped the oxygen mask over his head and

shoved it into the hands of a startled paramedic. He scanned the crowd, looking for anyone who would help. He spotted FBI Special Agent Finn Callaghan standing off to the side observing the scene.

Mateo knew how to track Sophia, but he needed help.

CHAPTER ELEVEN

Mateo didn't waste time on niceties. "We need to find Sophia. I mean Miss Reed."

Agent Callaghan stared at the fiery bank. A stark expression flickered in his eyes. "I'm sorry. I don't see how..." The tall, broad, serious agent rested against his AWD Ford SUV. He almost looked relaxed, but Mateo knew better. The by-the-book agent was tenacious and incisive. He had tackled corruption within the Granite City-Elkhead County Police Department without flinching.

Mateo grabbed Callaghan by the lapels. "Sophia thought the robbers would try and make their escape through the tunnels that run under the old city."

Callaghan gripped his wrists and shoved him back. He wasn't rough, but his actions were deliberate, telling Mateo without words to calm down. "There are tunnels under the city?"

He flexed his fingers, forcing himself to focus. "Apparently."

"You're kidding."

"No, she said she did a local history project in..." He waved away the thought. "That doesn't matter. What matters is she's still alive and she's wearing a smartwatch."

Callaghan straightened away from his vehicle. "Is it GPS enabled?"

"I believe so. It had texting ability. I need a computer with that app that finds lost devices."

Callaghan opened the door of his SUV and reached inside. "You'd need her password to make it work."

"I think she gave it to me."

Callaghan opened his laptop and then passed it to Mateo, who placed the computer on the driver's seat and crouched down. With a few keystrokes, he had accessed the app and typed what he believed to be Sophia's password, *auntvalerie1*.

He ground his teeth when the words *Incorrect Password* appeared on the screen.

He was on the right track. He knew it, but there could be several combinations of Aunt Valerie. Maybe Sophia had called her Val. No, she wouldn't have said *Valerie* if she didn't mean for the whole word to be used.

Who was Sophia? What did he know about her besides the fact that she wound him in knots? She was intelligent and observant. When working on a case, she inspected and verified every last detail. *Details...* She was a detail-oriented person. *Aunt Valerie will always be number one.*

That was it. She hadn't said Aunt Valerie came first. She'd said she was number one.

He typed *AuntValerie#1*. The app opened to reveal a pinging dot.

"I have her. She's moving." His pain and fatigue vanished as his heart pounded against his ribs. Sophia was alive. He would see her again. He wanted to collapse on the ground and pray, but he couldn't. It wasn't over yet. "She's in trouble. Old Woman must've taken her for a reason. He obviously doesn't need her as a hostage, so why would they burden themselves with a witness?"

Callaghan shoved him aside and climbed into the driver's seat. "I'll drive. You navigate, and on the way you can tell me about this old woman character."

CHAPTER TWELVE

Sophia climbed out of the cramped tunnel into a small, dark, musty shed. The smell of rotting wood filled the air. Through the open door she could see a streetlight and wondered whether it was past midnight. She itched to look at her watch, but daren't. Inviting their scrutiny would be foolish. With any luck, they would be distracted by the loot, and she could seize the opportunity to escape.

"Let's get everything loaded into the van." Old Woman turned on a flashlight, illuminating the floor. Scattered around the cramped interior were four large black tote bags, a small stack of gold bars, and three large backpacks. This was obviously the haul from the bank.

Baby did a little jig, dancing out through the open door and back in again. "We did it."

Old Man heaved a bag onto his shoulder. "I want the woman."

Bile rose, burning her throat. She instinctively stepped back, wanting to put some distance between herself and the rapist.

"And you'll have her as soon as the job is done, not before." Old Woman placed himself between Sophia and Old Man. The two seemed to be engaged in a childish staring match. She was grateful to have Old Woman's protection, if only in the short term.

Baby loaded his arms with gold bars. "I don't want her, and I think it was stupid to bring her." Then he turned his back and walked out carrying his haul.

She breathed a sigh of relief. None of this made sense. Why would Old Woman, who was clearly in charge, agree to bring her along? Eventually, they would have to kill her. She looked around the shed, searching for anything that could be used as a weapon. She squinted, trying to make out silhouettes in the murky darkness. There was some kind of tool hanging on the wall behind her.

"Are you going to stand and stare at me all night or get to work?" Old Woman snapped at Old Man who was still intent on outstaring his boss.

Sophia took another two steps back until her hand wrapped around the handle of what she hoped was a hammer. She gave it a tug, freeing it from the pegboard. There was a small crack as the old board gave way. She coughed, hoping to cover the sound.

"Okay, you win, but if you try to keep her for yourself, I'll beat you within an inch of your life." Old Man dragged a tote bag outside.

Old Woman turned to face her. "You can keep the wrench." He grabbed the bottom of his mask and tugged it over his head.

Her hand tightened around the metal grip. She didn't want to look. Seeing his face meant he would have to kill her, but she couldn't turn away.

She shouldn't have worried. His face was cast in shadows. She could make out the outline of his head, but that was all.

Old Man entered. "What the hell are you doing? She's not supposed to see us."

"It doesn't matter now."

The man who'd been disguised as Old Woman backed away, allowing Old Man access.

Her stomach felt like it had sunk to her knees, and she muffled a cry. Old Woman had lied. He'd said Old Man couldn't have her until they'd loaded their haul, and yet she could still see valuables, back-packs, and tote bags stacked near the entrance to the tunnel. The time difference between when she'd expected to be assaulted and now was probably only minutes, but she wanted to delay the inevitable as long as possible.

Old Man stepped forward as he tore off his mask, too. "This is like having Christmas and my birthday all rolled into one."

She edged back, but in the small confines of the shack, there was no room to maneuver. Her attacker had short pale hair on a large head with jug ears, and although she couldn't see his face clearly, she imagined he was salivating.

He grabbed her jacket, yanking it open. Buttons pinged as they hit the floor.

She swiped at him with the wrench, managing to hit him on the side of his head. He yelped as he stumbled sideways and then righted himself.

"You bitch." He fisted his hand and pulled back

his arm ready to strike.

Sophia closed her eyes and covered her head, waiting for the blow, but it didn't come. A sickening gurgling sound echoed through the night air. Old Man slumped onto the floor, clutching his throat.

Her heartbeat drummed in her ears. She gripped the wrench tighter.

"I've always hated rapists. I won't hurt you, but it's in your own interest to wait here until I call you." Old Woman backed away.

"W-who are you?"

He stopped before he reached the threshold. "I'm Ethan." Then he walked out of the shed. As he passed through the door, she noticed the glint of a bloody knife in his hand.

She exhaled, putting a hand against the wall to steady herself as her legs turned to jelly. He wasn't going to slaughter her...for now.

A sweet metallic smell filled the air...blood. Suddenly, her skin felt too tight, and she suppressed the urge to gag. Now wasn't the time to fall apart. She turned her gaze away from the dead body at her feet. Instead, she focused her attention on the haul from the robbery. Allowing Old Man access to her early was a distraction, another tactic, making it easier for Ethan to kill him.

Was Ethan murdering his cohorts so he could keep the money to himself? It wouldn't be the first time a criminal had massacred his partners, but that didn't explain why she was here. She had seen his face and witnessed a homicide. He would have to get rid of her. She needed to get out of here. Her legs felt heavy, as though they didn't belong to her body. It took all her willpower to force her feet to move.

She stopped at the door. Ethan was ten feet in front of her, crouching under the streetlight. On the ground next to him lay another dead body. She stepped forward. A warning screamed in the back of her mind, telling her to run, to try to get away, but the compulsion to see the face of the man she thought of as Baby overwhelmed her common sense.

"He was just a kid who liked shooting and blowing stuff up. He wasn't bad. He just got caught up with the wrong people." There was no emotion in Ethan's voice, no regret or remorse. He was simply stating the facts.

"Why did you kill him?" She wished she hadn't asked the question, wished she would have just turned and ran. But in her heart she knew that would never work. Ethan was a predator who was capable of hunting her down.

"I have my orders." Once again his voice was emotionless and flat, as though he had disconnected his feelings.

Sophia stared at the dead young man. He had a handsome face and shaggy hair. His skin was so smooth he looked as if he belonged in high school instead of robbing banks.

Ethan ran the tip of his knife over his victim's cheek. "Normally, I spend some time with my prey. I enjoy the feel of the blade as it splits the skin."

A lump formed in her throat. He was a sadistic bastard who liked cutting people.

He stood, still staring at the body on the ground. "Unfortunately, I have other things I need to do."

He strolled toward her, his movements unhurried and graceful. The light reflected off his balding head, his hair thinning at the front. She couldn't make out any other distinguishing features. His eyes looked brown, but blue eyes tended to appear dark at night so there was no way to say for certain. He could also be wearing contacts, but would someone wearing a mask go to those lengths? Maybe this guy would. He had calculated everything else, why not his appearance?

"I suspect your policeman boyfriend will be along to rescue you soon." He stopped in front of her, bent down to wipe the bloody knife on a mound of grass, and then sheathed it in his ankle holster.

"Mateo's still alive?" Some of her tension eased at the thought that this monster could be right.

Ethan shrugged. "That's my estimate. He might be a bit singed. If he's conscious, he would have told someone about your smartwatch."

She grabbed her wrist, feeling the device. "You know about that?"

"Of course. It was stupid of you to take the chance. If the others had seen it, they would've killed you, and there would've been nothing I could have done to stop them." He ran a finger along her jawline.

She stood still, too scared to react to his touch. She needed to concentrate. What was going on here? Most of the takings from the robbery were still in the shed. He hadn't made any move to load them into the van. Why had Ethan robbed the bank, taken hostages, demanded a ransom, and then set the fire?

She knew the answer to her last question. He'd set the fire so he could escape. And Ethan had his own reasons for committing the robbery. But there was one question she didn't understand. "Why did you take hostages and ask for a ransom? Why not just tunnel in at the weekend?"

"Think about it. I'm sure you can figure out the answer." His hand dropped to his side.

"The vault probably has motion sensors that are set once the bank is closed. If you'd burrowed in on the weekend, you would have set them off."

"Good job. I knew you were smart."

"But why the ransom?"

"Keep going, you'll get it." His voice held a mocking tone.

"You were always going to escape through the tunnels, but you needed time to break through the floor."

"Bingo." There was a smile in his voice. It reminded her of the patronizing tone a parent might use with a small child.

"And you had to kill them." She winced when she heard her own words. She'd meant to ask a question, but it sounded more like an accusation.

He smiled, looking normal, which was probably

the most terrifying thing about him, his ability to seem ordinary. "As a defense attorney, you should know you can't trust a criminal."

"A-are you going to kill me, too?" She didn't want to hear the answer, but had to ask.

"No." He tugged a bundle of folded papers from the pouch in his sweatshirt. "You'll need these." He stuffed them into her hand.

"What are they?" Sophia dropped the wrench and opened the pages, trying to make out the words in the dim light of the streetlamp.

"It's an insurance policy. There are a group of businessmen working together. They burn each other's buildings for profit. What do you lawyers call it? Ah, yes, a criminal conspiracy. They've been using the safety deposit boxes to communicate."

"Who are you?" She had a hard time believing he was some misguided Robin Hood.

"I told you I'm Ethan. Ramirez will have heard of me."

"Why are you doing this?" The lawyer in her wasn't satisfied with his answer.

"I had my orders."

"You can't have known I would be in the bank." She tried to imprint every detail about him to memory, knowing she would be questioned about this encounter for days if not weeks.

"No, I was supposed to visit you in your apartment tonight."

A chill edged down her spine. "My apartment?" He knew where she lived. It was a nice building with excellent security, or so she'd thought. She would have to move.

"Yes, now if you'll excuse me, I need to leave. Don't follow me." He ran a finger down her cheek. "Your skin is so silky. It would be a pity to scar it."

Once again she steeled herself, forcing her body not to respond.

Then he turned and thrust his hands in his pockets as he strolled to the end of the street. To a passerby, he might look like someone out for an evening walk and not a criminal who had just committed a bank robbery and stabbed two men to death. He whistled a slow tune when he reached the corner and turned right out of sight. The whistling continued for a few minutes, ringing out in the still night air, and then everything went quiet.

Sophia glanced at the body on the ground and then at the van that was supposed to be their getaway vehicle. It was partially loaded with their haul. The rest of the plunder was still piled in the shed. Ethan hadn't wanted any of the money or valuables. He'd engineered the heist just to get his hands on the documents and deliver them to her.

She needed to find Mateo. She had to know if he was alive. She took one step away from the body and then another.

A dark SUV pulled up next to her. Had Ethan changed his mind and come back to kill her? She grabbed the wrench from the ground. There was no way she would make it easy for him. She might not win, but she could fight. She would make sure there was evidence, blood, fingerprints, and hair, anything the police could use to identify her killer.

A tall fit man climbed out of the vehicle. She gasped, taking in the dark hair, the bruised face, and the torn shirt, but her mind couldn't absorb what she was seeing. Could it really be Mateo?

He stopped two feet from her. "Are you going to hit me?"

She dropped the wrench and ran to him, throwing her arms around his neck. "You're alive."

CHAPTER THIRTEEN

Exhaustion dragged at Sophia, making even walking a chore. The sun was rising over the city skyline by the time she left the Granite City-Elk-head County Police Station. Captain Tate, who was in charge of the investigation, had questioned her for hours. She'd handed over the evidence Ethan had given her after getting Mateo to make photocopies for her. Mateo had wondered aloud if Ethan's criminal conspiracy was linked to the arson case he'd been investigating. He'd come to her office on Thursday because he thought the teen, Ty Washburn, who was accused of Arson, was innocent. Could it be that the businessmen implicated in the documents had set him up? She would look into the matter...later.

It seemed the tunnels were now common knowledge. Granite City had let them fall into decay, but they could no longer be neglected. Sophia would have liked to see them restored, but now that they'd been used in a crime, they would probably be filled in.

FBI Special Agent Finn Callaghan had sat in on the interview. He had been particularly interested in Ethan. Both investigators were relentless, going over every detail again and again. Eventually, she had insisted they allow her to go home. She wasn't a suspect. She was a victim and a witness, and they had no right to hold her. She had every intention of cooperating. After she got some rest and a change of clothes, she would return to answer more questions.

Mateo drove her to her apartment. She was grateful to have him with her, and not just for safety reasons. Although, if he hadn't returned with her, she would've asked for a police escort. Ethan knew where she lived, and she had no doubt he could access her apartment at will.

She also needed to see Mateo and touch him; just knowing he was okay was a comfort. Every time she glanced at him, she said a prayer of thanks that he was alive.

Could he leave behind years of resentment? She didn't know, and she didn't have the capacity to think about it. Tomorrow she would wake up and face whatever the future would bring.

He walked her to her door. Taking the key from her hand, he unlocked it and went in ahead of her. She stood at the threshold, unable to do more than watch as he searched every room and checked the windows to make sure they were secure. Her home had always been a sanctuary, but not anymore.

Her place wasn't huge, or fancy, but it was cozy and had all the amenities she needed. There was a small kitchen with a laundry room attached. A living room with a gas fireplace, and two bedrooms, one with an en-suite bathroom. Another full bathroom was positioned near the front door. Pale morning light streamed through the patio doors that led to the balcony from the living room. It was hard to believe everything that had happened in the last twelve hours.

"All clear." Mateo ushered her in and closed the door behind her. A dark circle shadowed his one good eye. With the beating he had taken, she marveled he was still standing.

"You should go to the hospital." He had done his duty and seen her home safely. Now he could leave and get checked out.

She didn't wait for him to answer but instead walked to her room, shedding her clothes along the way. Ridding herself of the bloodstained and torn pantsuit was suddenly a priority. She had tolerated it through her interrogation, but now that she was home, she couldn't stand it a moment longer. She turned the water on in the shower, making it as hot as she could take it, and stepped under the spray.

Finally, she was alone and could release her fear, anger, and her absolute revulsion at witnessing two murders. Standing under the water, she allowed the horror of the day to wash over her. She felt the tension ease from her spine, but flinched when the cascade touched the bruises on her face. An unwanted sob erupted from her throat.

Suddenly, the curtain was pulled back, and Mateo climbed in. He stood before her naked; bruises covered his abdomen and his discolored face. His right cheek was swollen and tinged with purple, black, and blue. A small cut sliced his lip and another dissected his right eyebrow.

"I don't want…" She couldn't think about sex right now. She was too raw. Her emotions were stripped bare, as bruised as her body.

"I know." He wrapped his arms around her. "I thought I'd lost you." He ran a hand down her spine, soothing her, offering her the support she desperately needed. She knew she shouldn't trust him. In the morning, he would be gone and they would go back to being acquaintances who exchanged a polite nod in passing. But tonight her nerves were frayed, as though every bit of strength she possessed had been wrung out of her, leaving her ragged and worn.

"I'm just…" She was just what? How could she articulate her devastation? She couldn't. She'd met enough victims to know that time would reveal the long term effects of her trauma—and his trauma.

He kissed her hair. "Let me stay. I won't be able to sleep unless I know you're safe."

He grabbed her body wash from the side of the tub and squeezed a large amount into his hand. He worked the liquid into a lather and then said, "Turn around."

She did as she was told, thinking he needed some privacy. Firm, soapy hands caressed her neck, working down her spine in a circular motion. He seemed absorbed with covering her with suds. He lifted her arms one at a time and used the same gentle caress all the way to her fingertips. Then he knelt behind her and soaped her legs. For a moment the image of Old Man searching her body resurfaced, but he banished it when he said, "Face me."

She obeyed.

He worked his way up her body, paying special attention to her breasts. Finally he held her close and stepped back with her, placing both of them under the full force of the spray to rinse off.

Now it was her turn. Making sure to use an extra helping of body wash, she started at his neck and worked her way to his shoulders. His tattoos were fascinating. Gray roses spiraled down his right arm and stopped at his elbow. In the center of his back was an image of Lady Justice, holding a scale in one hand and a sword in the other. She scrubbed them clean and then worked her way to his butt. She lathered a soapy trail between his legs.

He sucked in a breath, cursed, and turned to face her. His erect penis nudged at her leg. "Honey, if we keep going, my dick is going to take control. I don't think either of us are in any shape to deal with that right now."

She held his battered and swollen face, his rough stubble prickly against her palms. "Are you sure you don't need to go to the hospital? I can drive you."

She wasn't sure she had enough strength to drive anyone anywhere, but she knew enough about him, remembered enough, to know he wouldn't ask for medical help unless he really needed it.

He shook his head. "No I just need to hold you."

She shut off the water and then nodded.

He grabbed a towel from the rack and rubbed her body, drying her. She stood watching, feeling detached from reality. He was alive. He had survived the beating and the fire.

She made her way to her bedroom and grabbed a nightshirt from her bureau then tugged it over her head. It was really just a large misshapen T-shirt with a frayed hem that came down to her thighs. But it was the most comfortable piece of clothing she owned. Then she climbed into bed and lay on her side, curling into a protective ball.

The mattress sagged as Mateo sat on the edge next to her. Beside him on the nightstand was his gun and badge. He must've put them there before he got in the shower.

He lay on his side and looped his arm around her. Then he rearranged their bodies so she was nestled in the crook of his neck. Light from the rising sun bounced off her dresser mirror, illuminating her closet door. Once again, she was struck by how familiar everything felt, which was at odds with her feelings. Her world had been upended. She was no longer safe in her own home. On the other hand, being here with Mateo seemed normal as though this was where he was meant to be.

Once again, a warning echoed through her mind. She should tell him to leave. He would break her heart. She was a defense attorney and he thought of her as the enemy. But she kept silent. After everything that had happened, she wanted him here.

When she woke up, he would probably be gone, and she would go on without him. She would find the strength to face the world with a smile, even if it killed her. Maybe she should move away from Granite City...but she liked it here. She had built her practice, had a great working relationship with her colleagues, and enjoyed the vibrant energy of the city. Starting over would be a bitch, but she could do it...if she had to.

Mateo ran a finger over her forehead. "Stop thinking."

"I can't," she murmured, but her voice sounded sleepy. The noise of downtown traffic drifted into the bedroom. Her fridge hummed and the apartment building creaked. Beside her, Mateo's breathing grew even and steady.

She would deal with her future tomorrow. Mateo was with her, asleep in her bed, and that was enough for now.

CHAPTER FOURTEEN

Sophia woke to an empty bed. He'd left. She'd known he wouldn't stay, but couldn't stop the desolate ache that seemed to touch every ounce of her being. When they'd been hostage, he had tried to protect her. More than once he had put himself between her and the bank robbers. He was brave, caring, and like her, committed to the justice system. How could she not fall for him?

Her throat tightened. She wouldn't cry, not today. She refused to be a weepy shell, pining for him. Even if he was the finest man she would ever meet.

She forced herself to sit up and throw off the covers. In a perfect world, she could curl up in bed and hide, but that wasn't an option. Captain Tate and Special Agent Callaghan wanted to continue their interrogation. She'd told them everything last night, but they seemed to think she had additional information. She doubted they suspected her. It was more likely they wanted to go over everything she had told them and make sure she hadn't left anything out. Sometimes witnesses remembered details days or weeks after the event.

She also had to contact her office and have

Marlow Kelly

Jane reshuffle her appointments. Wait, was it Saturday, Sunday or Monday? She padded bare foot to the bathroom and found her smartwatch on the counter. It was three o'clock on Saturday. Good God. Their ordeal had started on Friday evening. By her estimate, it was close to midnight when Old Woman, who was really Ethan, had taken her through the tunnels. So she must have been interrogated until dawn that morning. It was hard to believe so much had happened since Thursday night.

She had bathed last night but hadn't taken the time to blow-dry her hair. It had dried naturally while she slept. One glance in the mirror told her it was a crazy mess, sticking up at odd angles as if she'd been plugged into an electrical outlet. Once again, the urge to go back to bed overwhelmed her, but she forced herself to climb into the shower. *Be strong.* Those words would become her new mantra.

Normally, she didn't bother too much with her appearance, especially when it came to dressing for work. It was actually better if she dressed down and wore one of her pantsuits. Some of her clients were just plain creepy. She'd learned over the years that a smart, professional, plain look worked better than words to convey the message that she was in court for business not pleasure. Today, however, she needed to feel attractive so she chose her sexiest underwear, a silk black matching set that included bra, panties, and garter belt. She covered them with a slim-fitting, black, sleeveless sheath dress. She even took the time to straighten her flyaway hair and apply makeup to cover her bruises.

A last look in the mirror told her that outwardly, at least, she seemed whole. She sucked in a breath and stood tall. At heart, she was a fighter. She would get through this.

The smell of coffee hit her the moment she opened her bedroom door. Had Mateo made coffee and then left? The nerve of the man. She stopped and listened. Someone was in the kitchen. Her stomach fluttered as she inched closer.

"There you are. I heard the shower and made breakfast. I assume you like eggs. They were in the fridge." He smiled, and her heart did a little flip.

"I thought you left." She stepped closer.

"I did. I had to go to my place and get some clean clothes. I hope you don't mind I borrowed your keys." The right side of his face was still mottled and swollen. He wore a white T-shirt that stretched over his taut muscles and revealed an intricate pattern of roses that swirled from his right elbow up and under his short shirtsleeve.

"That's not what I meant. I thought..." *You'd abandoned me.* There was no way she would say that aloud. She tried a different approach. "Why are you here?"

He removed the pan of eggs from the burner and turned to her. His appraisal was long and slow. His gaze took in her legs, working his way until his eyes met hers. "Wow, you look fantastic. I mean, you're always beautiful, but...wow."

She could see the heat in his dark eyes, and her

body responded. Her heartbeat raced. She licked her suddenly dry lips. A small voice in her head told her to resist, but that wasn't what she wanted. This was Mateo. The man who had put himself between her and danger, who had cared for her. Whatever had happened in the past was over. She could no longer hold on to her anger. She loved him. It was as simple as that.

He hadn't answered her question, but instead turned back to the stove. He picked up the frying pan and used a slotted spoon to divide the eggs between two plates that already held buttered toast. "You should eat, and then we'll talk."

She didn't want to eat. Her stomach was jittery and tense. The stress of the last couple of days and dealing with their growing sexual tension was too much. The robbery might be over, but she still had to cope with whatever was going on between them.

"Are you going to leave?" Part of her wished she hadn't asked the question. She wanted him to stay, even if it was just for a moment, but there was no way she could ignore her fears or the damage he would do to her soul if he left.

He stepped toward her. "I'm staying."

His voice was so low she wasn't sure she heard him. "What are you saying?"

Using his fingertip, he brushed her hair away from her face and tucked it behind her ear.

Her breathing hitched at his touch.

"We are going to go the distance. I mean marriage, children, growing old together, everything."

His hand trailed across her cheek, under her chin, and down her neck.

"You're going too fast for me." She swallowed and grabbed his hand. She couldn't think when he was stroking her, seducing her. More importantly, she wasn't sure she could trust this change of heart.

"You don't want children?"

"Yes...no...one day, but not today. And-and..." How could she explain how she felt without being completely vulnerable? "You don't like me."

He shook his head. "Yes, I do. Look, I get that you don't trust me. I was so focused on putting the bad guys away, I couldn't see the whole picture."

"I loved you...and you..." She closed her eyes. She didn't want him to see her pain, but knew it was too late.

He kissed her cheek. It was a simple peck, but once again heat flooded her body. She opened her eyes and placed her hands on his chest, feeling his warm muscles under her fingers. "Every time you're near, I want you to make love to me. Why is that? I wish things were different. I wish—"

He grasped her by the waist and placed her on the kitchen counter. Then he grabbed her ankles and folded them around his hips, securing his position at the apex of her thighs. "It's not the declaration of love I want, but it's a start. If sex is the only thing we have in common, then I'm going to take full advantage of it."

He grabbed her under the knees and slid her forward so her butt rested on the edge of the counter.

Then he slowly eased her dress up, scraping her sensitive inner thighs as his fingers traced her garter belt.

"Please don't send me away," he begged.

She couldn't respond. A shiver of pleasure racked her body. This wasn't fair. She was aroused, whereas he seemed to be in control, logical, and was using her weakness for his benefit. She reached between them and unzipped his fly, intending to excite him and level the playing field. But then his engorged penis sprang free. He wasn't as unaffected as she'd thought.

"You're not wearing any underwear." The words escaped her mouth before she could stop them. "Do you always go commando?"

He smiled as he flicked the crotch of her panties aside and brushed his thumb over her clitoris. "This is a special occasion." He kissed down her neck as his clever hands continued to excite her.

She groaned and threw her head back. Her breasts were sensitive, pushing against the confines of her bra.

Finally, his finger found her vagina. "You're ready."

She was sopping wet. "Take off my underwear." It was supposed to be an order, but sounded more like a plea.

He did as he was told, stepping back as he slid them down her legs. Then he shoved his jeans down so they pooled around his knees.

Once again he wrapped her legs around his waist,

leaving her open and defenseless, the tip of his penis resting against her opening.

He kissed her. It was a long passionate kiss. Their tongues twined, sending another frisson of pleasure cascading through her. She groaned into his mouth and eased forward. She wanted to feel him inside her, needed to impale herself onto his throbbing cock.

In one hard thrust, he was in her up to the hilt. He stilled. "Was I too rough?" His voice was strangled as if uttering the words had cost him.

"No, don't stop." She grabbed his butt, enjoying the feel of his smooth cheeks, and pulled him toward her, driving him deeper.

He cried out and thrust into her, plunging in again and again. He set a steady, unhurried pace. His mouth closed over her nipple. The sensation of him suckling her through the fabric of her dress pushed her closer to the edge.

She heard someone screaming, but it sounded far away, and then she realized it was her voice crying out, yelling one word over and over, "More, more, more..."

The rhythm changed, becoming urgent, harsher. He pounded into her. His cries matched hers as they raged on toward oblivion.

****

"Can a man die from too much sex?" The late afternoon sun cast long shadows across the room. Mateo's stomach grumbled, reminding him that neither of them had eaten. They had made love four times in a row, and he needed a break.

He hadn't meant for them to end up in bed, not this time. She'd been so shattered last night. He'd only intended to care for her, but they seemed to have an overpowering physical need for each other. "I shouldn't have judged you all those years ago. I should have taken the time to understand."

"Understand what?" She pushed up on one elbow so she could face him.

"That your work as a defense attorney is just as important as my work as a cop."

She smiled, a genuine carefree reaction, which made her green eyes sparkle. "Thanks."

"To be honest I don't know how I'm going to function as an officer of the law and be involved with you at the same time." He brushed his lips over hers.

She snuggled against him. "You'll manage."

He hugged her close, enjoying the intimacy of their pillow talk. "I'm not so sure about that. I was supposed to deliver you to the precinct to finish your questioning hours ago."

"The fact that you have brought up my interview with Captain Tate and the FBI contradicts the notion that you won't be able to function."

It was his turn to laugh. "I haven't even called them. I'm surprised they aren't hammering down the door."

She eased away from him and sat on the edge of the bed. Her gaze wandered the room and then focused on him. "I have to move. Ethan knows where I live."

He knelt on the ground in front of her, clasping her trembling hands in his. "Move in with me."

She considered it, her lips pressing into a thin line. He thought she would reject his proposal, but instead she said, "Isn't that a little fast? We haven't been on a date in twelve years."

"I can take you out if that's what you want. Where do you want to go?" He sat on the bed next to her, still holding her hand.

"A crowded place where we won't end up in bed."

"We don't need a bed to have sex. I mean, we did it in your office and on your kitchen counter. I can pick you up and take you to a fancy restaurant, but what's the chance we'll make it home? My car does have a backseat." He waggled his eyebrows and was pleased to see her blush as fear vanished from her eyes.

"We belong together. Stay with me."

"Are you sure?"

"I've never been more certain of anything in my life."

"Let's have a trial run. I'll move in with you, and if we don't kill each other in the next six months, we'll look at getting a place together. Deal?"

"Deal." He already knew he wanted her to stay forever, but if she needed time, that was fine. Blood engorged his throbbing penis as it sprang to life again. He leaned back, pulling her on top of him.

She straddled him, positioning herself so her legs were either side of his hips. His cock wedged against the opening of her vagina.

"Is this how you always seal a deal?" she panted as she eased herself onto him.

"Only with you." It was the last thing he managed to say before he was caught up in the maelstrom of their lovemaking.

CHAPTER FIFTEEN

Special Agent Finn Callaghan cracked open a beer bottle and took a long hard swig. None of his triggers had been activated while he was out. He double-checked the carpet. He always vacuumed before he left, being sure to brush the pile in the same direction so if someone stomped through his home he would be able to see their footprints in the rug.

His small rental was clean, sparse, and military neat. It would never be homey, but that was fine with him because he wasn't planning on settling down.

He set his beer on the counter and then pulled his fridge to the center of the kitchen, revealing a suspect board hidden on the wall.

He'd recently become aware of a group of businessmen who called themselves The Syndicate, which was a cheesy Hollywood name as far as he was concerned. He suspected they were using violence and manipulation in order to protect their financial interests, but he couldn't be sure of their real objective. He had no proof or leads of any kind.

He also believed they had a mole inside the Department of Justice, one who had accessed his personal files and shared them with businessman, Lance Ackerman. Ackerman had tried to use the information to blackmail him. It hadn't worked, but the whole thing set off Finn's alarm bells. Something nefarious was going on, and he needed to figure out what it was. He had the feeling that a countdown had started. He just didn't know what the crime would be and who the suspects were.

Any sensible man would let it go, but he couldn't. It wasn't only the injustice of a group of rich businessmen controlling events, killing innocents, and doing whatever necessary to consolidate their power; they had tried to kill his friends. This was personal.

He took another swig of his beer and studied the photos and facts arranged on the wall. He wished he could have discussed the details with his partner, Kennedy. She knew of their existence because she'd worked the Quinn and Morgan cases with him. But he had decided to shut her out. It wasn't that he couldn't trust her. She had proven she would do the right thing no matter what the cost, but he wanted to protect her. She was a young agent with a bright future, and he was risking his career and maybe even his life.

He moved Ethan's card to the center of his murder board. He had no doubt Ethan was an assassin for The Syndicate. The big question was why did they want to expose an arson scam in Granite City? The obvious answer would be that it threatened their interests, but he had no idea what those interests could be.

He took another drink. The syndicate had come to his attention when one of their members, Marshal Portman, had tried to blame his friend, David Quinn, of kidnapping and murder. They had surfaced again when they had tried to acquire Molly's Mountain, a property that bordered another friend, Tim Morgan's, land. The Syndicate hadn't initiated Tim's legal troubles, but they had sent Ethan to murder the local police chief and then tried to frame Tim for the crime. That plan was thwarted by pure dumb luck.

He considered his suspect list, people who he believed were part of The Syndicate: Marshall Portman, Lance Ackerman, Brad Harper, Ethan Hunt, and Lucy Portman. Of that list, only two of them were still alive, Lucy and Ethan.

His superiors had told him to back off where Lucy was concerned. He understood, even if he didn't like it. She had money, connections, and a high-priced lawyer. As far as law enforcement was concerned, she was in the clear. If he was going to go after her, he needed irrefutable evidence, and that was in short supply.

Ethan was another matter altogether. Finn suspected he was a hired thug who had murdered the police chief of Hopefalls in the grizzliest manner possible. And now he had shown up again, the mastermind behind a successful bank robbery, but Ethan's only goal was to attain evidence of a criminal conspiracy. He hadn't even taken the money. It had been recovered along with the contents of the safety deposit boxes.

Sophia Reed's description of him was a little off. She had said he was balding. Just four months ago, Tim had described him with short, thick hair. Finn eyed the composite picture of Ethan. He had a plain face. It would only take a few small tweaks to change his appearance.

He cursed and pushed the fridge back into place. He would question Sophia again tomorrow, but he suspected it would be another dead end. All he could do was wait until he surfaced again. Sooner or later, Ethan would make a mistake, and when that happened Finn would interrogate him. One day he would get the answers he needed.

For more of these characters set in The Gathering Storm series, check out Sun Storm, Fire Storm, *and* The Wedding Deception.

ABOUT THE AUTHOR

After being thrown out of England for refusing to drink tea, Marlow Kelly made her way to Canada where she found love, a home and a pug named Max. She also discovered her love of storytelling. Encouraged by her husband, children and let's not forget Max, she started putting her ideas to paper. She enjoys writing suspenseful, fast-pace romance stories that always feature strong women.

Marlow is an award-winning author, and a member of the Romance Writers of America.

For more information about Marlow's books visit her website at http://www.marlowkelly.com

You can also check out Marlow's Amazon Author page
https://www.amazon.com/Marlow-Kelly/e/B00MZE72CS